ALSO BY BETH NUGENT

City of Boys

Live girls

Live
girls

CCL

A NOVEL BY

Beth
Nugent

Alfred A. Knopf   New York   1996

THIS IS A BORZOI BOOK
PUBLISHED BY ALFRED A. KNOPF, INC.

Library of Congress Cataloging-in-Publication Data
Nugent, Beth.
Live girls / by Beth Nugent.
p.   cm.
ISBN 0-679-41978-0
1. Young women—United States—Psychology—
Fiction.   I. Title.
PS3564.U347L58 1996
813′.54—dc20   95-36148
CIP

Manufactured in the United States of America
First Edition

The author would like to thank the National
Endowment for the Arts, the Colorado Council on
the Arts, and the Rocky Mountain Women's
Institute for their support.

Live girls

My sister never slept. This is what she always told me: she never slept; she never had a dream; she never thought of me. Any of it could have been true. I never saw her sleep. When we were children, she moved around our room at night like an animal in the dark, a little creeping thing, stealing from shadow to shadow. She was like a shadow herself as I watched her through half-closed eyes, a moving patch of fluid darkness. Some nights, I woke to find her beside my bed, her hand on my face, brushing softly over my skin like the hand of a blind person, as if to search out some sense in the shape of my cheek, the curve of my lips. I could smell her skin, hear her intent little animal breath, a faint damp wind across the desert of my face. I longed to open my eyes and look at her, but at even the slightest motion she pulled her hand back and retreated into the darkness. So I lay still and did not flinch, even as her fingertips brushed across my eyes; her touch was like the most fragile of insects lighting a moment on my face—a soft pulse of wings, then flight.

Some nights I only dreamed she was there; I would lie for long minutes, following the map her hand made of my face, until suddenly there would come a cough in the corner, or a sigh from across the room. I dreamed we would be there forever, together, in the dark. I dreamed she would never leave me.

I dream of her still. There are nights I wake to a hand on my face, and I think: She is here now. I can feel her hand, her breath, I can almost see her face, but when I open my eyes there is nothing but the shape of my own dark room, and the hand on my face is my own. It is my own touch I feel, my hand flutters at my face like a moth beating against the window. My heart is a moth, fluttering against the walls of my chest; it is a living thing in my throat.

I have not seen her face for years. She moved out of our room some time before I left, but even before that, years earlier, she had begun to hide her face, draping her hair across her cheek or holding her hands in front of her. Sometimes when I think of her, all I can recall are her hands, the long white fingers, the delicate bones. When she died, I thought: Now all I have is what I can remember.

I stop at the curb for a car to pass, and glance into the window of a bar. In the dark glass, my face is featureless, a blank circle of flesh atop a body.

When the car passes, I head for the theater. The marquee is dark, and from here, several blocks away, the woman on the poster in front is beautiful, her lips a bright-red bloom in the middle of her face; only as I come closer can I see her tongue between her parted lips, like something peering out from the dark hole of a cave. Her head is huge, three or four times the size of my own, and though I know it's a trick of the picture, I feel her eyes on me as I unlock the doors to the theater.

I leave the marquee dark, but light up the lobby and turn on the popcorn machine; it gives out a lame little buzz as the light at its base flickers, then settles into an unsteady greasy glow. Though the machine is empty, the oily yellow smell spreads quickly through the lobby. I take my place in the ticket bubble. Dave will be here soon. My face floats in the dark glass and I stare out at the street through my mirrored eyes. Men pass by, glance in at me. Their eyes linger a moment on my face before they move on. I am here to be seen.

After a while, Dave shuffles into view a few blocks away, carrying a black plastic garbage bag full of popcorn—it's already popped, soggy and stale, like something left over from another theater. "Pre-popped" is what Dave calls it. He gets it from an outlet somewhere, he says vaguely; it's cheaper and cleaner than popping it here, and besides, he always adds, no one ever buys it anyways. He only offers it because people like to smell popcorn when they go to the movies, as though our customers are ordinary moviegoers, as though what we show are ordinary movies.

He stops at a corner to wait for a car to pass and rests the bag on his feet, though it can't weigh more than a pound or two; he crosses the street, then drags the bag behind him the rest of the way, bumping it up and down over curbs like a sack of laundry, not like anything he is expecting people—even in the abstract—to eat. He'll dump it in the machine to warm it; then I'll sell maybe a bag or two, eat a bag or two myself. When I go home tonight, the machine will be full, and when I come in tomorrow, it will be empty again. We never talk about what he does with it. He could throw it away; he could scatter it in the alley for the pigeons and the rats; he could give it to bums in the street; he could get rid of it in any number of ways. He himself hates popcorn, he says; he hates the smell of it, and the taste, and the way it feels between his teeth, and I believe him, but recently it occurred to me that he waits until I've left, then eats it himself. It's not his nature to throw away something he's already paid for.

As he approaches the theater, I look down, and, when he raps on the glass by my head, I jerk with a feigned start, as if I have been concentrating on something. He stares through the glass at me for a moment, then turns abruptly toward the doors.

—Popcorn, he announces as he enters the lobby. He lets go of the bag and leaves it in the middle of the room, like a tail he's just shed, and as I come from my ticket bubble to the counter, we share our usual awkward moment; though I am here every night, he always seems a little surprised to see me, and a little uncertain what to do about it. I am not the kind of girl he usually hires. He looks at me a moment, then gives me a tight little smile.

—Machine on? he asks as he turns to retrieve the popcorn.

—It's broken, I say. —You know it's broken? And he stops; he knows it's broken.

—It's fine, he says.

—No, I say. —It's burning everything.

He stares at me a moment, the muscles in his jaw working, then looks at the machine. In the past few weeks it has begun to overheat, scorching the bottom layer of popcorn to a black little strip that runs evenly around the bottom of the machine like a layer of sediment. The burnt greasy smell of it gets in my hair and clothes and skin. I smell it when I fall asleep at night; I smell it the moment I wake up. It is becoming the way I smell. Dave sighs and shakes his head.

—Christ, he says, then comes around the counter to the machine, approaching it warily, as if it is a wily and experienced enemy he has battled for years. He stops about a foot away and reaches his hand out to touch the glass tentatively, then looks at me. —It's warm, he says.

—I know. I turned it on.

He crouches, and I crouch with him, as if we are examining a complicated piece of sophisticated machinery, rather than a box of metal and glass that does nothing more than heat whatever is put inside it. Dave taps the machine gently on the side and gazes unhappily through the cloudy glass. After a moment, he unplugs the machine, then plugs it quickly in again and straightens, looking at his watch.

He glances anxiously at the door; the first show will begin soon, but so far the only people who display even an idle interest in us are two old queens parading by. They stop to examine the poster outside, and when they see Dave and me inside watching them, they blow us kisses, then clutch at each other with false little screams, their bright-red lips pulled back from their teeth.

—Faggots, Dave says. —You go away.

He says this almost absentmindedly, more to himself than to them or me, and with no apparent rancor.

He gazes at them as they wander off down the street, then he turns and retrieves the popcorn from the lobby, dragging it across the floor, then lifting it high to dump the popcorn into the machine.

—Okay, he says, nodding at the popcorn machine. —See how it works now.

—All you did was unplug it, I say. —I could have done that.

He gives me an irritated glance.

—I suppose, he says, —that a college degree makes you an expert in electrical engineering? He shakes his head. —This isn't just some piece of junk, you know. It's a very delicate machine. You could have broken it.

He puts his hands on either side of the machine, then suddenly lowers his head and lays it down on the machine, closing his eyes, his ear and cheek against the glass. His face goes dreamy and quiet, almost serene. This is an expression I've never seen on him; usually he is tense and suspicious—he looks at you a long time when you say something, as if he is trying to figure out the secret meaning of whatever you've just said; then he takes a drag of his cigarette, and says yeah, well, and comes up with some kind of response. He has a tight guarded face—the kind of face you would expect to find on a man who killed his wife, which is exactly what he is. It was an accident, of course, something to do with camping or hunting or fishing, something he could not have helped, but even so, it shows in his face as if it were a murder he'd planned and executed. It's not something you might guess about him at first, but as soon as you heard it, you'd nod your head and think: Of course. There is something hunted about him, furtive and criminal, as if he has some sense that things might seem more or less fine now, but one day he is going to round a corner and there it will be waiting for him after all these years: his punishment. In the meantime, he has married again; he has a new wife, a new house, a whole new life built right over the shattered foundation of the old one, but he seems to take no pleasure in it, or in anything else, approaching each moment like another in a long sentence he wishes neither to continue nor to end.

I watch his face. His eyelids beat gently, as if he is sleeping. The machine is hot. I suppose he is thinking about killing his wife. It's hard to imagine what else there is for him to think about, how there could be room in his brain for something other than that—for any other act than that, for any other face than hers, for any other thought or word or idea.

—Well, I say, —you could be right. He opens his eyes and looks sideways at me, his cheek still pressed against the machine. —But you know, I go on, —it's asking a lot from me, to sell tickets and work the concession stand both.

He closes his eyes again, not even bothering with a response; we both know that I spend most of my evenings here reading magazines. Sometimes whole nights go by without a single bag of popcorn sold, and those I do sell usually turn up full at the end of the evening, abandoned here and there under chairs around the theater. Apart from Dave, I may be the only one who actually eats it. The only other food here is a half-empty shelf of candy left over from some earlier time. What we have is what never sold—Dots, Jujubes, ancient fruity stuff that's not worth the trouble it takes to chew it. When I came here, it was all stacked up against one side of the shelf under the dusty glass, making you wonder what you had missed by coming so late. I opened a box of Dots, and the candy inside had fused together into a single colorful lump that had stuck to the side of the box. I closed it up and replaced it under the counter, then dusted off the glass and arranged the candy in even little stacks along the shelf, so that they looked like something someone might actually want, but so far I have not sold a single box.

Dave sighs, his eyes still closed.

—What the hell, he finally says. —We don't sell any popcorn anyways.

He lifts his head from the machine and stands, blinking. His cheek is red from the warm glass.

—It's just one more thing I can get rid of, he says.

He has a long list of things he can get rid of. I am on it somewhere. In the short time I have been here, he has got rid of several things already: a soda machine; a velvet rope that used to stand in the lobby; afternoon shows; the afternoon ticket taker. He is left with fewer and fewer things to give up, and as business daily dwindles, I watch his eyes move around the theater, roving from unnecessary object to unnecessary object, wondering of each: is this something he needs? until finally his eyes settle on me. I am usually idle at such times, leaning back, reading a magazine, and when I become aware of him watching me, I try to look busy. I straighten the few objects in my ticket bubble; I run a napkin over the counter; I look impatiently out the window at passing men, willing them to stop and buy a ticket from me, and all the while Dave watches, wondering if he can do without me.

And meanwhile, each night there are fewer customers, most of them more or less undesirable. There is usually a handful of sailors from the submarine base, and sometimes a couple of underage high-school boys from the suburbs, but most of the men we get come from what Dave refers to as an aging customer base–tired old men with no friends and small pensions who want nothing more than to be left alone to sit in the dark for a few hours watching women on a screen. The more desirable customers–younger men, who bring life and friends and money into a place–don't bother with us; they all would have come in here once, Dave tells me, but now things have gone all to hell; half the men are fags, and the rest go to places with live girls–bars, clubs, strip joints.

Dave watches them as they pass us by, shaking his head. He is not happy. This is not the life he had expected. The life he had expected, he told me not long after he hired me, was a life of art; he said art the way some people say God, or love, with a kind of fearful devotion, and a distant lost look in his eyes. He told me he wanted to show the kind of movies that only a few people would understand and come to see. I pointed out to him that he wasn't really so far from that–he was showing movies that anyone could understand, but still only a few people came to see them. He gave me an annoyed look, then lit a cigarette and stalked over to the doors, where he stood and smoked, staring out at all the men who passed us by. This is not what he wanted to do, and he is not even making a decent living at it. Every night, he runs the film for three shows, and while a few men sit in the theater and watch it, he sits in his office and dreams of art, thinking of how things would be if they were different from this. And now all he can do in the name of art is show what he calls "quality films"–he calls all of our movies "films"–which to him means movies with plots. Oh, he'll say, musing over a movie brochure as if it were a museum catalogue, this sounds kind of interesting, and then he'll read out loud a description of some skeletal plot, usually involving women home alone, surprised by mailmen or metermen or plumbers, and usually ending with something like: Hot Action Ensues. He puts little red checks by the ones that interest him—usually those with the most complex plots. He seems to think this might make a difference to our customers, though from what I can tell by looking at them, plot would be little more than an unwelcome distraction. As they head into the theater, they do not have the faces of men looking for plot; they have the faces of men looking to see something happen and not worry too much about how or why or to whom. But it matters to Dave, and he has done his best, though lately he has had to downscale even here, ordering more and more of what he calls lower quality films, which, he says, are cheaper to rent; this used to bother him, but lately he seems less and less to care, really, as if every day he is losing a little more heart.

—Hey, he says, —things are tough all over, and he tells me that I of all people should know this, me with a college degree. I do not have a college degree, but Dave thinks I do. It is why he hired me. The other girl who worked here, and we were both called girls, though she was in her forties, did not have a college degree. Her name was Patty, and she always wore something shiny—a shiny shirt, or scarf, or sweater. Everything she wore was shiny, but it was cheap, so that after only one or two wears, the metallic threads that made it shine started to pull away from the fabric, sticking out all over like little wires. It made her look like something that had been clawed by a cat. She had mean little lines around her eyes when she looked at you straight on, but if you ever caught her just sitting staring out into the street through the bubble, her face was slack, her eyes gone soft in a kind of milky daze.

It's been only a month or two since Dave let her go; she has probably already found another job, but whenever I think of her, it is always sitting alone at the window of a rented room somewhere, staring out at the street while her shiny blouse catches bits of sun and reflects them uselessly back into her room. When I think of Patty is when I feel most powerfully a desire to leave here, to get on with the life that it is not too late for me to have. I feel it waiting for me sometimes, my life, crouching like a beast in the trees, patient and inevitable.

Dave brings it up regularly, the life he thinks I should have. I am better than this, he tells me; I have a college degree. I have options, he says, and though he is vague about what exactly they might be, sometimes when he brings them up, there are moments when I almost believe in them myself, when I begin to think of my life as something different from what it is and what I expect it to be—but even at these moments, I am unable to settle on any particulars. I have options, I say to myself, but when I close my eyes and try to imagine what they are, what I see is what is in front of me: a bubble of glass surrounding me on all sides. My sister would laugh. What kind of options could I possibly have, she would say, someone like me?

And so, lacking a clearer picture, here I stay, despite the options Dave is certain I possess. And he is torn: he likes having me here. He has never hired a college graduate before, and he thinks I add a touch of class to the place. He actually said this: a touch of class. He is willing to bet, he says every so often, that he owns the only adult entertainment center in the whole city that employs a college graduate. He has deep respect for the education he thinks I have, often asking me my opinion on things I don't even think about, things like politics and world affairs. Sometimes he even asks about the movies he picks; he likes to get a woman's-eye view, he says, and every now and then he lays a catalogue almost diffidently in front of me, and together we stare down at it as he muses over the possibilities. He murmurs through the synopses and I look at the pictures—always of women, either undressed or in some kind of elaborate underwear outfits, strappy things with garters and lace and holes cut out. Dave turns the pages thoughtfully, giving me time to muse with him, as if we are looking at a garden catalogue, planning our summer bulbs together. He does not appear to think of art at such times; his eye is on the bottom line, and as long as there is some semblance of plot, it's all the same to him: X, double X, triple X—he considers the options as would any businessman.

—Lots of heavy S & M, he'll read, then look up at me and ask what is the woman's-eye view on that. I shake my head and ask him what does he care, since women do not constitute a large part of our customer base. —Yeah, he says, and looks back at the brochure.

What women we do get are usually professional dates—hookers gliding in on the nervous arms of young sailors—though, from time to time, a suburban couple wanders in; while the men buy the tickets, the women always hang back, as if they are not part of the transaction, and they eye me covertly, then look quickly away when I meet their eyes. They are used to seeing women like Patty in places like this, not someone like me, who looks so much like them.

When they come out, they leave quickly, without another glance at me, their eyes on the backs of the men with whom they came. I do not seem so respectable to them as I do to Dave—but to him we are the same; he looks at them and he looks at me, and he knows I do not belong here. This is no place for someone like me, he says, and every day that I spend here causes the future he thinks I should have to slip further and further into some dark distance out of my grasp. We watch it disappear together, as though we are staring after the last train he was supposed to put me on, and when it is gone we will turn to one another, whose company we must continue to share, and wonder: What now? The remorse it causes him is remorse enough for the two of us, but still it is a remorse he clearly thinks I should share, and sometimes when he talks about my options, I feel as if we are two friends sadly shaking our heads over the sorry fate of a third. As long as I am here, he feels some complicity in my fate, as if I am just another crime for which he must atone. I am his responsibility now, and as my prospects continue to recede, he is showing the strain. Sometimes I can feel him standing in his office door watching me. If business remains slow, he cannot keep me, and yet how can he let me go when I am so unwilling to explore my options?

Lately he has taken to bringing in newspapers, then leaving them on the counter, folded open to the classifieds. Usually I ignore them, but I picked up one a few days ago to see that he had gone through and drawn neat red boxes around several help-wanted ads, all for jobs requiring skills I don't possess: secretary, administrative assistant, even dental hygienist—respectable jobs, suitable for college graduates. I thought for a while of what it might be like to have one of those jobs, to get out of bed every morning and stand in front of my mirror thinking: I am going to my job as a dental hygienist. I could not get past the mirror. I turned the page and came upon the personal ads, which Dave had also gone through, though the marks he left here were fainter, made with a pencil. The few I read were all from men who described themselves as professional. Most of them were seeking same: women who were educated; women who were attractive and lively; women who had options. I wondered what it would be like to meet these men, what we would do, and talk about. I have had so few conversations.

None of the men he had marked were the kind of men I would meet in a place like this, and I closed the paper and went into my bubble. Outside, the sky was flat and growing dark, the street flat and growing dark, the light and the people and the cars—all flat, all growing dark. When Dave came along and saw that I had left the newspaper, he glanced at me, then stuffed it into the wastebasket. He has not brought in another since, but his increasing agitation makes me uneasy. Sooner or later, something is going to have to be done about me. But for tonight, another show is about to begin, and Dave glances at the doors, then gives the popcorn machine one last slap.

—Well, he says gloomily, —show time.

He unlocks the doors and steps quickly aside, as if to brace himself for an onrush of anxious customers, but it's several minutes before the first sidles up to my bubble for his ticket. They will drift in and out until we close; most come in clumps at the start of each show, but a surprising number wander in and out throughout the evening, with little regard for the show times printed on the placard in my window. Dave takes this personally, given the effort he has made to provide movies with clear beginnings and ends, but he has little leverage: it is not a seller's market.

—Customer, he says now, jerking his head toward the ticket bubble, and I take my seat there, smiling at the man outside, who ignores me as he shoves his money through the slot and takes his ticket. Most of my transactions are like this, with neither a word nor a look exchanged, but every now and then someone stares right at me, and lets his gaze linger, and in his eyes I can see the creepy hope that I am part of the price of a ticket. Sweetheart, he will call me, and bring his face so close I can see the tiny hairs beneath the skin on his face. I smile; I smile at them all. Dave has instructed me to do so; it's bad enough, he says, that the poor bastards have to come to a place like this for their entertainment, someone might as well be nice to them. And being nice to them is clearly not a job he himself wants to take on; most nights he stands in the lobby watching them enter, shaking his head sadly as they walk by, as if they are cows off to the slaughter. Lately he is becoming almost belligerent, snorting loudly as he expels a cloud of smoke, occasionally even leaving the lobby to start the movie before the last man in line has bought his ticket. If they do not care about the trouble he goes to to entertain them, then let them miss the beginnings of the stories he has provided; it is nothing to him, and if one or two of them get a thrill from leaning their hungry faces close to mine—well, that too is nothing to him; there is an inch of glass to protect me, and as the days pass, there is less he can do for me. He has other things to think about.

Several men have formed a ragged little line in front of my bubble, and Dave watches them from the lobby; he lights a cigarette, drops the match on the floor, lets his ashes fall on his shoe. He stares gloomily out at all the men who pass us by; he doesn't care who they are or where they are headed–all he knows is that they are taking something away from him. The man in front of the line pushes his money through the slot, and leaves his hands on the ledge, his fingers trembling. I look to see his face, but his head is down, bent so low I can see a spray of purple bumps on his scalp, under a fine haze of hair. He does not look up to take his ticket or his money and he keeps his head down as he enters the theater. Dave watches him go in, and when the last customer is inside, Dave stalks across the lobby and heads upstairs to start the movie. This week is something with a Western theme; the picture in the brochure was of a woman wearing only cowboy boots, a hat, and a gun belt, leaning back on a bed. She held a gun between her legs. Dave was intrigued by the Western motif.

—What do you think? he had asked, showing me the picture.
—Everyone likes a good Western. Even women like a good Western, don't they? he asked, and looked at me. I nodded and said that yes, as a rule, even women liked a good Western, and he put a little red check beside the picture. As the last customer slips inside the theater, I hear the music start up, and under it the clatter of hooves.

Until the next show I have nothing to do but sell a few tickets, and I sit back with one of the magazines Dave brings from his house; every month or so he carries in a new stack, mostly things like *People* and *Reader's Digest*. In the corner of each cover is a neat rectangle where the label has been cut out. It's hard to imagine Dave reading a magazine; it's hard to imagine him anywhere other than here, doing anything other than this, but here are these magazines as proof that he leads some sort of life. Sometimes I like to think of Dave's wife, whom I have never met, sitting in a bright sunny kitchen, a cup of coffee cooling at her side as she cuts out the subscription labels.

I wonder if she thinks of Dave's first wife, if she looks around uneasily when she senses Dave in the room behind her, if she jumps at sudden noises, or if, unthinking, she brings her hand to her throat as Dave lifts a knife to carve a roast, feeling the cold slip of the blade against her own skin. She must pause, from time to time, in her task of removing labels to lift her head and drift off into the thought of what it must be like to be killed by Dave, until some suburban detail—the step of the mailman, the cry of a child—pulls her back to her work, and she bends to it again, carefully lining her scissors up evenly with the label.

It may be that she never thinks about Dave's first wife, never considers how he killed her, never wonders what she is risking. I could think of nothing else, nothing but when he would kill me, and, possibly, how. It would seem only to be a matter of time, and I would keep track of where he was at all times, what he was up to. Even here sometimes, I look up to see him standing in the lobby gazing at me absently, and I cannot stop myself from thinking: How long has he been standing there? What might he do to solve the problem I have become to him? And then he will shake his head, flick the ash from his cigarette, and offer up some harmless comment about the weather before he heads back to his office.

I learned about his wife from Patty, who told it to me one afternoon when I drifted in early, with nothing to do before my shift. I stood in what I hoped was a companionable silence at the counter while she sat in the ticket bubble ignoring me. When I came around the counter to get a bag of popcorn, she turned her head slightly.

—You know, she said, —he's not a saint.

I nodded, though I didn't know who she meant. This was the most conversation we had ever had.

—I know, I said as I got my popcorn. When I turned back from the machine, she was still turned toward me. The sun was behind her and her face was a black shadow in the light. I smiled.

—Who? I said.

She snorted and turned back to stare out the window, her hands placed neatly on the ledge in front of her. This was all I ever saw her do there, sit and gaze out the window. There were never any customers for the afternoon shows; until Dave hired me, I suppose she worked the evening shift as well. She bothered him; he told me once that he wanted someone more lively, who was willing to smile at the customers, who would make them feel glad they came. Patty did not even look at them. She looked only at the street. She could do a whole transaction—money, ticket, change—without shifting her gaze. Sometimes when I came to work I walked right past her in the bubble, but her eyes never moved to follow me. Once, I stopped, stood right in front of her; our faces were a foot apart, with only an inch of glass between us. It was like looking into a mirror, the way her eyes stared right back at me but didn't quite see me. I don't know what it was she saw. There is nothing to look at but a long row of run-down hotels and bars, but she used to gaze out at them as if she were gazing into a field full of flowers.

Now she sat completely still, her head a dark blot; all that moved was a long silvery thread from her sweater that waved gently up into her stiff blond hair. I wanted to walk over and smooth it down for her, but her shoulders looked as rigid as wood and I stayed where I was, assuming our conversation had ended, until she turned again to face me, jerking around as if someone had taken hold of her shoulders and was forcing her to look at me.

—He killed her, she blurted, then brought her hand to her mouth and looked, stricken, at Dave's office door, where she kept her eyes as she told me what little I know. As she spoke, I realized that she loved him, which made me sorry for her; I knew even then that he was going to have to let one of us go, and that it would be her. When she finished, she turned back to look out the window, at the bleak landscape in front of her; perhaps she saw Dave as she contemplated the burnt-out faces of strangers—gazing at them, dreaming of him. One day he would come to her: a soft step behind her, hands on her shoulders, head bent to hers in a soft kiss. I don't really blame her for hating me, what I took away from her.

When Patty told me about Dave, I could see that she despised me for listening, and after that she never really looked at me again. She kept her eyes straight forward even when we passed to change places in the ticket bubble, as if there were something to look at just past my shoulder.

When she was here, the bubble always smelled of her: her perfume was something flowery and cheap; it hung in the air behind her, a lingering scent of desperate romance. And she filled the bubble with things: a little ashtray from Florida with an alligator perched on the edge, though she did not smoke; a coffee cup with *Patricia* written on one side, and *Las Vegas* on the other; a little snow bubble with a tiny Statue of Liberty inside. I always meant to ask her if she'd been to all those places; she did not strike me as the kind of person who traveled. She had also taped to the window a picture of a German shepherd, cut from a magazine, and I did ask her about that, if she had a German shepherd of her own. She looked at me with a kind of scornful pity. —No, she answered, as if I had asked her if she'd been to the moon, as if to own a German shepherd were the grandest of dreams. No, she said again, and turned, then touched the picture with her finger; it was a friendly-looking dog, the kind that looks like it's smiling when its mouth is open. I asked her what was its name, and she turned and looked at me a long time.

—Andy, she finally said, and turned back to the window.

Live girls

When she left, she packed up all her things in a shoebox and brushed past me without a word, as if it were just another shift change. Though we were not friends and she did not like me, I liked having her here; perhaps it was just her things, the evidence of her presence. Now that she is gone there is nothing here but me. Her scent lingered a few days before I noticed that it too had gone.

I put my nose to my arm and breathe in: skin, popcorn. It is the skin that smells of popcorn, or the popcorn that smells of skin. I missed the picture of the dog. I had begun to think of it as a real pet, one we all shared, though we never saw it. I used to think of him living in Patty's room, sleeping at the foot of her bed, waking her up in the morning for his walk. When his picture was gone, I felt as if something I loved had died. I put up a picture of my sister over the tape mark that the dog's picture had left; it is the only picture I have of her, caught by the camera before she could turn completely away from it. Her hand is raised to cover her face, leaving exposed only a bit of her jaw and her eyes, fixed angrily on whoever was taking the picture. It might have been me. I told Dave it was a picture of my roommate from college, and when he asked why her face was covered, I told him she was shy. He said whoever it was, she looked crazy, and after a day or so I took the picture down. I put it in the drawer under the register, thinking I might want to put it back up on the glass sometime, but when I came in the next day it was gone. In its place, I tape up pictures I cut out of Dave's magazines—sometimes cats or dogs, usually people. I leave the pictures up until their faces become so familiar I find myself thinking of them when I am not here, looking for them on the street, sometimes even dreaming about them. Then I take the pictures down.

A few days ago, I put up a picture of a family standing in front of a van they are advertising; they seem to be in Arizona, or New Mexico, some desert place with mountains rising up behind them. There is a mother, a father, a small boy, a small girl. All of them are smiling. There is nothing at all dark in their faces, nothing to trouble them; when they sleep, they awake refreshed, and if they have dreamed, they do not remember their dreams.

These are the people, or people just like them, I think about when I write my family; I imagine these people, or people just like them, receiving my letters, missing me, wondering when I will return, and when I do return, these are the people who will be waiting for me. They will smile at the sight of my face. They are thinking of me right now. Right now my sister is at her window; she is staring into the dark trees; she is thinking of me. I close my eyes. Bees are buzzing at my heart. Bees are swarming in my head; I can feel the poke of their tiny legs on the surface of my brain. The things I believe are not true.

I look down at the magazine in my lap; faces I recognize are spread across the cover: movie stars, singers, entertainers. I have never seen them, but I recognize them all. As I flip the pages, I hear Dave creeping up behind me, and I keep my head down, but glance up at the ticket window to see his reflection in the glass; he stops, stares at my head, waits for me to turn to him. I flip the page to a new article, and he sighs; after a moment, he gives out a little chain of escalating coughs, until finally I meet his eyes in the glass.

—So, Karen, he says, and I turn. Karen is what he calls me, though my name is Catherine. Either he heard it wrong when I first introduced myself, or he prefers to call me Karen—and because he pays me in cash, there have been no written transactions between us that might point out to him his error. I am becoming used to Karen, and, really, Karen seems a more appropriate name for someone who works at a place like this—it is more casual somehow, less serious than Catherine. Karen is who I am now, or who I am becoming, while Catherine waits quietly in a dark room without doors or windows. Her eyes are covered; her mouth and ears are covered; her hands are buried in sand. She feels nothing. Spiders skitter over the ceiling, and up and down the walls.

—So, Karen, Dave says again, and looks around the bubble, glancing a moment at the picture of the family taped to the window. He drops his cigarette on the floor, steps on it and grinds it out, then looks suddenly down in dismay. The carpet is spotted all over with little scorch marks where he has dropped his cigarettes; usually he bends quickly to retrieve the butt, and rubs at the burn, but now he just stares down, then looks back up at me, running his hands over his head.

—So anyways, he says. —My wife's sister's kid might be stopping by.

He looks abruptly around behind him, as if someone there has said something, though we are alone in the room. He sighs.

—I told him to stop by, he says.

He brings his wife's sister's kid up from time to time, and this is always what he calls him—his wife's sister's kid, never his nephew, never by name. Lately he has brought him up more often; clearly he sees him as a prospect for me, and apparently the only one, since he is the only man he has ever mentioned. He said once that he thought his wife's sister's kid and I would have great chemistry.

—Chemistry? I said, and he rolled his eyes and said, —Yeah, look, just do me a favor and meet him, okay? And I saw that his wife's sister's kid was not only a prospect for me, but that Dave was looking for someone for him as well. I asked him why he hadn't introduced him to Patty, and he looked blank a moment at the sound of her name, though she had worked for him for more than ten years, and then he said, —Oh yeah, Patty. Well, they wouldn't have hit it off.

He waits now for my response, and I glance down at the magazine in my lap. On one side of the page, two movie stars are entering a restaurant arm in arm, while on the other side, a crowd is lined up watching, a sea of faces I do not recognize, their eyes focused on the movie stars. My sister kept a picture of this actress tacked to her wall, and I think of cutting this out and taping it up here in my bubble, next to the family with the van. Dave clears his throat and leans forward, then repeats everything he's just said about his wife's sister's kid stopping by, as if perhaps I have not heard him, then he stands back up straight.

—You know, he adds. —Just stop by. He waits another moment as I look back at the picture, and he sighs. —His name is Danny, he says, and I look up.

—Well, I say. —I'm kind of busy. I *am* at work.

Dave glances at the magazine in my lap, then puffs a little air through his lips and stalks to the glass doors, looking out. After a moment, he presses his face against the glass, peering out as far as he can see without opening the doors, then glances around at me.

—He should be here by now, he says. —He's usually a pretty reliable kid.

On his way back to the counter, he stops to dig at a scorch mark in the carpet with his toe, then shakes his head and looks up at me, his toe still stuck in the rug.

—He works for the city, he tells me hopefully, and watches me as he waits for my response. Finally I say okay, which seems to be enough, and he heads back to his office, but every time I get up to go to the bathroom or get a drink of water, he glances sharply out at me, as if I might be trying to escape.

The evening passes like every other: outside, men pass by; they glance in at me, sometimes say things I can't hear, then move on. Outside my bubble, they pass like weather, storms moving across glass. I lay my head down. My heart is a moth, beating against the walls of my chest. My throat is a moth; my brain is a ball of spiders, moving, walking; a ball of moving spiders moving.

The glass rattles beside my head, a hand rapping against it.
—Hey, someone says, —hey sleeping beauty. I open my eyes to
a greasy face only inches from mine. He grins. —Two, he says.
A hooker stands behind him, and together they head into the
theater.

Outside, everything is quiet, the sidewalks empty but for a boy
sitting on the bench across the street, gazing at me with the
fixed, anxious look of someone who's been waiting a while. He
is clean-cut and beefy, wearing a shirt that I can tell even from
here is either new or freshly pressed. I watch him over the top
of my magazine. Every now and then, he stands abruptly and
starts to cross the street toward me, then stops before he
reaches the curb, and throws himself back down on the bench.
He must think that because I am so brightly lit up here in my
bubble I can't see him, though he is only thirty or forty feet
away. He is too clearly out of place here to be anyone but
Danny, Dave's wife's sister's kid. Every few minutes he looks
down at his knees and lets out a sigh that lifts his whole body,
then lets it fall. Then he looks back up at me, stares a while,
stands, stumbles back, and so on.

After a while, a tall transvestite drifts by, slowing to eye the boy.
He passes, pauses, circles back, pauses again, then perches delicately on the arm of the bench, looking coyly up and down the
street, as if he's waiting for a bus. The boy freezes, locking his
eyes on me, as the transvestite gently eases down on the bench
next to him. He smiles at the boy, says something, then reaches
his hand toward him, but the boy rises abruptly and, with one
last desperate look in my direction, turns and takes off. The
transvestite stands, calls out something, then shrugs and drifts
languidly away, his purse dangling at his knees. I have seen him
before. I feel sometimes that I have seen everyone before.

The streets are empty again when he's gone, my only company
the family smiling down at me from their van. They are a per-

fect group, the four of them; a perfect group that needs nothing. A pet, perhaps, is all they lack, and as I flip through another magazine, I keep my eye out for a picture of one, a dog or a cat. Not both. I do not think there would be room for both. Andy would have been the perfect pet for them, sturdy and big, a good traveling pet.

When the show ends, Dave comes out to watch the audience leave, blinking like rats in the sudden bright light, curled into themselves like rats, scuttling away like rats. One of them stops at the counter and stares at me until I come over to him. His face is pale, and there are black lines where his teeth meet his gums. He comes here often.
—Listen, he says, his eyes moving around the room; he twists the tail of his coat between his hands.
Dave has spotted us talking and drifts over to protect me; he likes me to keep my interactions with the customers at what he calls a professional level–smile at them, he says, don't have conversations. The man turns to him.
—Listen, he says. —Some kid in there–he jerks his head toward the emptying theater–some kid in there took my watch.
Dave looks at him, and the man glances away, looking nervously around the lobby, patting at his wrist, then looks back at Dave, who sighs so dramatically that even the customer can see he is annoyed.
—Some kid, Dave repeats, —took your watch. He shakes his head. It's not an unusual complaint: once or twice a week a kid comes in to hustle after hanging around out front a while, making himself obvious; then he lingers in the lobby until the five or ten or fifteen customers have all had a chance to see him; then he follows them inside. There are boys like this on every corner, some of them as young as thirteen or fourteen. They all look more or less the same, like hungry kids who have never had anything they wanted. Dave pretends not to notice them when they come

in, and together we pretend not to know what it is they are doing; once they get inside, they stay for all three shows, and make what they can, although, given what Dave refers to as our customer base, it can't be more than twenty or thirty bucks. So things disappear—watches, rings, wallets, even an occasional overcoat.

The customer stares at Dave, waiting for him to do something, and Dave points at a small sign by the door, printed with the usual disclaimers about valuables.

—See that? he says, and the man's lips move as he reads the sign; he looks back at Dave, his face uncomprehending, and Dave sighs again, almost patient. —You sit by who you sit by, he says, and shrugs in a friendly way; the man looks at him a moment longer, then a sudden anger flashes in his face. Dave steps back.

—Hey, he says sharply. He puts his hands up. —Look, he says. —You sit by who you sit by.

He heads for his office; the customer turns to me, but I avert my eyes and back away from him toward the bubble, leaving him stranded at the counter, looking back and forth between Dave and me as we move away from him. When he finally leaves, Dave turns at his office and watches him go. He lights a cigarette, drops the match.

The customer stops outside on the sidewalk, the fingers of one hand circling his wrist; he gazes one last time at us before he walks away.

—Poor bastard, Dave says. —Poor stupid bastard.

He shakes his head, then looks out the window at the tiny clump of men waiting to buy tickets for the next show. —Jesus Christ, he says; he heads up the stairs to start the next film before I have even sold a ticket to the first man in line.

As I sell tickets, I glance up at the family with the van; the man's watch is safely strapped to his wrist. Where they are, no one can take it from him. In a moment, they will all get back in their van and continue their vacation, stopping along the way to see things: the Grand Canyon, the Painted Desert, Mount Rushmore, the kinds of places from which Patty collected souvenirs, the kinds of places that are familiar to me, though I have never seen them. They will drive, and will not stop until they reach the water's edge, where they will stand together in front of their van, gazing out at the bright sea. They are a happy family. Wait for me, I want to call to them. I'm coming, I want to say. Outside, men in line shift impatiently from foot to foot while I fumble with their tickets and their change.

As the evening passes, I search through magazines for a picture of a dog, which is what I have settled on for the family in the van, something large and friendly; a Saint Bernard perhaps, or a golden retriever. I begin to consider appropriate names. *King*, I write in the margin of a magazine article. *Rex. Spot.*

At the end of the night, Dave comes out to watch the sparse crowd leave; last to emerge is the kid who probably stole the watch earlier. He is just a boy, almost too young to shave, his cheeks and chin wisped over with a delicate young beard, and he slouches out, hands in pockets, eyes on no one. I turn out the light in my bubble, and when everyone has gone, Dave locks the doors, then looks up and down the street again; the customers are gone in a minute, scattering like cockroaches. Dave shakes his head.
—I don't know where he was, he says. —Maybe something happened to him. He's not really all that smart.
He looks at me speculatively. —You didn't see him, did you? Big kid? Brown hair?
—That could describe a lot of people, I say.
—Well, he says doubtfully, looking back out at the street.
—I'm not sure you'd really notice him if he did show up. I don't know if he'd exactly stand out. He's just a big kid, kind of goofy-looking.

He looks at me quickly. —In a nice way. Goofy in a nice way. You know.

—I know, I say. —Goofy in a nice way.

—Right, he says. As I come around the counter, he backs against the doors, his arms spreading like wings at his side to block my way. I stop.

—I don't think he's coming, I say, and he looks at me a moment, then steps aside so that I can leave.

—Yeah, he says, then, —Listen. You want me to walk you?

He offers this every night, and every night I say no, I'm just going for coffee. He nods.

—Well, okay, he says. —But watch it. The streets are full of nuts.

He lets me out and locks the door behind me; the marquee goes dark before I've even begun to walk away, casting me into sudden shadow.

By the time I reach the corner, I am sure Dave is already at the popcorn machine, and as I round it, he is filling his mouth with popcorn; he can hardly stand to chew it, but he fills his mouth, swallowing greasy handful after greasy handful until he reaches the burnt layer at the bottom, where he pauses a moment to look down at it before he eats that too, even as it turns to ashes on his tongue.

The streets are still, dead in the hour or so before the bars close, and there are only a few men out on the street with me, their coats buttoned up against the damp chill of an early winter off the ocean. Winter here is bleak and chill and dreary; there are weeks of no sun, and nothing but gray: gray sky, gray water, gray wind. You could walk into the water and think it was the wind. A chill rises up around me; I cannot spend another winter here. I will spend the next winter of my life somewhere else, someplace clean and bright and warm; I will explore my options.

And then, when I have gone from here, I will hardly even remember it. Oh yes, I will say one day, if I happen to hear the name of the city; oh yes, I lived there once. I will laugh. If you could call it living, I will say lightly. It will be a past that isn't even a part of the woman I am going to become, this city. It will disappear. It has practically disappeared already, all on its own; it is hardly anymore even something you could call a city; rather, it is just another grimy Eastern seaport collapsed in on itself with its own inertia, caving slowly into the dark heart at its center. It is a city full of rooms that rent by the week or the day or even the hour, and it is populated by the kind of people who would rent them; there are no families here, and no houses, and every day what respectable people there are move farther and farther away, where there are houses and families and re-spectable jobs and hobbies; they live in little developments built just for them, spreading outward from the city, like spores cast away from a plant. The city they leave behind them is a city of misfits, and it exists more and more to meet their misfit needs. Everything is ending here: buildings crumble even as you pass; sidewalks crack under your step, and everywhere you look are the faces of missing persons. They stare out at you from flyers, or grocery bags, or posters flapping against fences, and in big letters under their faces they wonder: HAVE YOU SEEN ME? They are usually children, though some of the pictures are seven or eight years old, that's how long they've been missing. By now, they will no longer resemble their pictures on the fly-ers, and so much time has passed that even if they did turn up, there might be no one left still looking for them, no one who would bother to come and get them. And you can see it in their faces, even in the faces of the very young, some sense that this will be their fate—to end up missing—that at some point, not far off in their short futures, whoever it is who is supposed to be watching them will turn away—for a second or a minute or an hour—and then they will be gone. And this is the kind of place they turn up in. Cities like this are meccas of missing persons, crawling over and over one another like bugs in a jar, and everyone here has the same look, the resigned, blotted-out eyes of people who are missing or disappeared or turned away from, people who are just watching things happen, even when they are happening to them.

They are people without options in a city without options, a city that has nothing going for it but its past, and even that cannot save it now. There is not much left besides the college and the submarine base, and the base will close within the year. Demoralized sailors from its dwindling forces spend more and more of their time here in town, wandering around drunk and aimless, with glowing white heads from being so long under water, shut away from light. They float in and out of bars like strange radioactive bulbs. They can see their futures right in front of them, in the faces of old Navy men who ended their duties here and never moved on.

The college is up on the hill to the east; once a private women's school, it long ago closed, changed hands, and reopened as a religious college. Half of its buildings are closed and shuttered, and the student body is just a tiny group of girls who wander around the deserted grounds like the last nuns in a dying convent. I spent a year there, sent by my mother, who had attended it herself twenty years ago, when it was a real college. She was there only a year or two herself, before she met my father, married, had us. She seemed to think she had left something there, something she was meant to have, and that it was still there, waiting for someone to retrieve it and return it to her—some life different from the one with which she had ended up. It didn't occur to her that time might have changed things; the school and the city were to her little more than fond memories and missed opportunities, and she sent me off with a long list of places to go, things to see and do. I went to two or three of the places on her list. The pizza parlor she recalled as a college hangout was a bar. I went there in the middle of the day, and when I opened the door, a rectangle of light stretched across the floor to the bar. I stood in the open door, half-blind a moment, dazzled by the glitter of dust in the light; as my eyes adjusted to the dim interior, the faces of a few old men sitting at the bar took shape; they were staring at me. I smiled and stepped back onto the street, closing the door in front of me. Later I wrote my mother that it was just as she had described it. *It was full of college students,* I wrote; *we all shared a pizza. The owner was very nice to me,* I told her; I said that he remembered her. *I go there often,* I added. These are the kinds of things I write about; when my sister was alive, I wrote often to tell them how well I was doing, how many friends I was making, how much at home I felt.

I spent my first several months at the school in the corner of a room with a girl who was younger than I, but who had already given herself to God. She spent most of her time on her knees, staring up at the sky, where she believed God was, gazing back down at her. At night I woke to her untroubled breath in the bed across the room, and I used to lie awake and marvel at how easily she could sleep so close to a stranger. She always dreamed of God, she told me once, and every night before she went to bed, she prayed, asking God to watch over her while she slept. I asked her once what would happen if God fell asleep, and she looked across at me on my bed with my book, and shook her head sadly, as if I alone was not aware of some basic fact of life that everyone else in the world knew.

—God never sleeps, she said, and turned back to her prayer, but for a moment a shadow of trouble had crossed her face; it was the only one I ever saw. She opened her eyes. —And if he does, she said, —he dreams of us.

And so she slept, dreaming of God dreaming of her. She slept deeply, in almost total silence, but somehow it was more disturbing than my sister's prowling, and some nights I got up and stood at her bed, watching her, to see what it looked like to dream of God, to be dreamed of by God. In the light that came in through our window, her face was at perfect peace, a tiny pale moon glowing in the light of the moon outside.

After a while, she moved into another room, with another girl. They were always together, and whenever we passed in the hall, they both gave me smiles full of distant charity, then exchanged a look of pity before they moved past me.

After that I spent most of my time alone in my room, while every afternoon on the large grassy lawn outside women gathered to pray and sing, all holding hands and staring at the sky. I watched them from my window. My roommate was always right in the middle. She had sung in her church choir, she told me; her minister told her she had the voice of an angel. *I joined the school choir,* I wrote in a letter home. *Everyone tells me I have the voice of an angel.*

I used to wonder what my sister made of my letters, if she ever read them. I liked to think of her creeping down at night to search for a letter from me, to snatch it from the wastebasket and carry it back to her room to read. She would have rolled her eyes at the things I wrote about—making friends, going places, meeting people. They are things she would have known I could not have done.

There was never any question of sending my sister to college; it would never have occurred to anyone to suggest it, and what would she have done there had she gone? She would have sat in the backs of classrooms, her face hidden by a book, or she would have walled herself off alone in her room. She would never have done the things I write about.

When I returned here from my sister's funeral, sometime in the spring, I left the school, and as I descended the hill in the old car my parents had sent me off in, a rattle began somewhere underneath me, and worsened as I drove. I stopped at the first gas station, and the men there, figuring me for a college girl, quoted me a price I could not pay; I thanked them, and drove back into town, where I removed the license plates and parked in a tow zone, then sat at a doughnut shop across the street, waiting for someone to come and take the car away. A cop was there in a heartbeat, then a tow truck, and as the driver hooked up my car, the counterman leaned forward on his elbows and watched with me. He told me a story, which he swore was true, about a man who ate a car. It was a Buick, the counterman thought, and it took the man several years to eat it, grinding it up piece by piece, mixing it with food. He was trying to set some sort of record, and he ate every part of the car, not just the body and the engine, but the windows, the door handles, mirrors, seat cushions, all of it. Not a piece of that car went to waste, the counterman said and shook his head in awe, though he had clearly told the story many times. Then he fell silent, staring out the window, until the cops came inside the coffee shop. He gave them some doughnuts as I watched my car bounce off behind the tow truck, whamming into the road at every bump; it had let me down, but still I was sorry to see it go. It was the car I had grown up with; I wondered for a moment what it might have tasted like. Perhaps someday I will write my parents and tell them that I have eaten it. I will tell them it tasted like chicken.

When my car disappeared around a corner, a man sitting on a stool next to me rattled his cup in his saucer and said, —Those bastards, apparently speaking to no one, but I turned to look at him anyway. It was Dave. I told him that had been my car, and he looked at me a moment, then offered me a job at his theater. Just "his theater" was all he said, not what kind of theater it was. I told him I was just finishing college and had planned to leave town, but maybe I'd take him up on his offer until the job market improved. He nodded, impressed. It was our first conversation and almost nothing I told him was true, except my name, which he got wrong.

I have never been back to the school, though I can see it just by looking up from the window of my room. It runs smoothly along without me. The girls there never venture beyond its neat grounds, and the cross in front looms over the city like a constant reproach. I have been gone only seven or eight months, but even in so short a time there are things I am forgetting. My roommate's name. The way my room looked. The books I read. The things my roommate said when she prayed. I can remember only a few things: the way her face looked when she slept; the sound of her breath in the dark room; the hum of her voice as she prayed before she went to bed.

Sometimes I find myself thinking about some place I have been, the people I have met there, and I wonder how they are, until it occurs to me that it's just a place on my mother's list, a place I have never been. I still have the list, and from time to time I start a letter describing another visit to another one of them, but then I lose the letter, or forget to mail it. There are several yet to go—a zoo, an ice-cream parlor, a scenic overlook.

It takes me only a few minutes to walk to the Hygienic, the diner halfway between the theater and my room. It's open all night and all the after-hours lowlife come here when the bars close. This is what Dave calls them.

—I don't see why you want to hang around with that lowlife, he says, shaking his head sadly. —You with a college education. I could make you some coffee if you want coffee so bad, he offers occasionally, but I tell him I like being around people before I go to bed, and he shakes his head again, thinking of all the ways he ought to be saving me from all of this if only he did not want so badly for me to stay.

During the day, the Hygienic is full of cops and old men, but at night it's lowlife: junkies, drag queens, hookers, drunks. I arrive early and the place is slow, so I have a booth to myself. A few of the other booths are occupied, mostly by mismatched couples brooding over coffee as they stare away from each other. A row of junkies is at the counter; they come here to eat whatever sweet thing they can stomach between fixes, trembling over huge banana splits or giant gooey Danishes, then washing it all down with glass after glass of Coke. Their faces are orange under the bright light, and they pause occasionally as they eat to glance around them, scanning the room with that driven junkie urgency, always on the lookout for the next thing to ingest. They come early, to get a seat at the counter, and always sit at least one stool away from anyone on either side, avoiding even the chance of accidental physical contact with another person. As the place fills up, they grow edgy, and by the time the first wave of transvestites arrives, all big hair and waving arms, they begin to leave, sliding down from their stools one by one to slip away.

This is not the kind of place my mother thinks I frequent. Here the tables are always sticky, even when they've just been wiped, and the yellowish walls are covered with panels of aging spotted mirrors; long spidery cracks crisscross the silver under the glass, and in some places it is worn away entirely in big black patches. As you pass it, your reflection cuts in and out—there you are, then you're gone, then there you are, back again.

Outside, the bars are closing and the after-hours crowd is beginning to filter in: first are the ex-sailors, milking their meager pensions—they drink all day in cheap bars, then come here to avoid returning to their rooms. They are interested in no one, not even each other. We get a lot of them at the theater; some of them come in every night. If they recognize me here, they show no sign of it. They sit hunched over coffee, looking straight ahead at nothing. In the mirror, they look like a row of dead men; all that tells you they're alive is that occasionally the waitress comes by and refills their cups.

After a while, when the action on the streets dies down, the hookers wander in, for coffee or dates or whatever they can find, and after them the transvestites from the drag bar. Rounding out the crowd is the usual assortment of drifters, who come and go with no one noticing, men who are everywhere but seem at home nowhere; they are moody and always look slightly soiled and slightly hurt.

I sit by myself and drink coffee. Sometimes, looking around the room, I run into my own reflection; it used to give me a jolt to see someone I knew, but lately I've found myself watching my own face for a moment or two as though it were the face of a stranger, and wondering what someone like me is doing in a place like this.

The place is mostly full when Jerome makes his entrance, bursting through the door in an explosion of color, all bright yellows and purples and pinks. The few junkies left at the counter jerk down from their stools and creep away as he brushes past them, drawing his pink scarf across their bony backs. By now, all the booths in the place are taken, and in a moment he is looming above me.

—Honey, he says, —you've got the only free booth. Do you mind? He joins me and orders coffee, then looks carefully over all three pages of the menu, though he comes here every night and every night orders the same thing: either a small bowl of wax beans or a diet plate with cottage cheese and lettuce. Once, in a reckless moment, he asked for an English muffin, which came with a little packet of grape jelly. He opened the jelly and looked at it, then closed his eyes and touched his tongue to it gently; then he sighed and put it back on the plate. What little he ate of the muffin he ate dry.

When the waitress brings his coffee, he orders wax beans and I ask for a doughnut; then Jerome closes his menu and looks around. He has a pleased, satisfied look on his face—perhaps at having a booth nearly to himself, perhaps with the bright-pink sunburst he's dyed into his hair.

He stirs a packet of Sweet'n Low into his coffee and gazes around at the other transvestites, his eyes traveling up and down their long bodies, and after he has scrutinized them all in the bright light and has satisfied himself that he is, for now, the most beautiful, he sits back and lets his eyes fall with mild indifference on me. I don't know what he sees when he looks at me. I am less interesting to look at than most of the women here, and he would probably prefer me to be more glamorous, more capable of drawing men's eyes to us.

One night not long after I had met him, he took me by the elbow and said, —Girl we got to do something about you, then took me with him into the women's room, a dank little closet with barely room for a sink and a toilet. He stood me in front of the mirror and crowded in behind me; side by side in the glass we looked like two different species. He sighed, then set his huge purse on the toilet and began pulling out makeup, then set to work on me like a professional, maneuvering around me in the tiny room, his face only inches from mine as he applied a delicate line to the top of my lip. I closed my eyes while he worked; his hands moved across my face like a flurry of wings, quick and delicate. I could feel the muscles behind my eyes beat as he brushed shadow across my eyelids. He was so close I could smell his skin beneath the scent of his perfume. When he was finished, he was quiet a long time. I could hear him breathe.

—Well, he finally said, —now you're beautiful, and I opened my eyes to a face I had never seen before; it was the face of a beautiful woman, a face that people would turn to watch on the street. I stared at myself, then met Jerome's eyes in the mirror. He held our gaze a long moment before he broke it, and in that moment there was something familiar in his face; only later did I realize it was the look I had seen on my sister when she sat on her bed and watched me comb my hair, or stood behind me in the bathroom as I brushed my teeth, her eyes running over and over my face as if I could not see that she was watching me. What was in her face was not just jealousy and not just hate, though they were there, but something else—something like the way hungry people look at food, or the way a person who is all alone stares after a family.

Jerome swept his makeup back into his purse and left the bathroom abruptly, but I stayed, looking at the face in front of me: this was the woman I should have been becoming, I thought; this was a woman with options. I stayed there in front of the mirror until someone rapped at the door. I looked around for Jerome when I came out, but he was gone, and I finally found him standing out on the sidewalk, talking to a man. He did not look at me when I passed him. I did not wash my face when I went home, and I tried to sleep lying on my back, but when I woke up, the makeup was nothing but greasy black and red smears across my pillow. I stopped at the store that day on my way to work, but there was a whole wall of makeup, and I could not remember the names or colors of anything that Jerome used. I used to buy makeup for my sister, on her birthday, or at Christmas, little cheap tubes of lipstick or eye shadow. She always took it from me as though someone were forcing her to, but sometimes at night when she thought I was sleeping, I would hear the rattle of the little drawer where she kept it, then a long silence as she used it. In the dark, she was only an outline; the most I could see of her was the dark shadow that stared out from the mirror. Jerome has never offered to make me up again, but sometimes when I watch his long dark hands stroke his coffee cup or dismantle a packet of Sweet'n Low, I want to close my eyes a moment and remember the way they felt when he touched me.

He takes a sip of his coffee and finishes his survey of the room, then looks at me.

—So, honey, he says. —How's business?

—The same, I tell him. —Slow.

He shakes his head. —Girl, he says, —you got to get with the times. Get some new movies. Them old straight things is lame.

—It's not my theater, I say. —I don't really have any say in what we show.

—Uh-huh, he says, his eyes drifting over to a boy who is walking slowly between the booths up to the counter. Several men in the room have their eyes on him, and he walks slowly, showing off what he has to offer. Sooner or later, he knows, one of them will be desperate enough to offer him some money, something to eat, a place to spend the night. He is very pretty, with the darting black eyes that come from always looking for a home in the faces of older men. When the boy reaches the counter and sits down, Jerome turns back to me.

—Uh-huh, he says again. —Well, that's okay.

This is typical conversation for us. Whenever no one attracts his attention, he turns back to me, asking odd impersonal questions, the kinds of questions you find in magazine interviews with celebrities, which is probably where he gets them–questions like what was my most embarrassing moment, or what three words would I use to describe myself, or, once, what kind of tree would I choose to be. He usually tells me his own answers to the questions before I have even thought of mine. I was still wondering about the tree question a few days later when I heard him ask it of a boy at the counter. The boy looked at him and said he didn't know the names of any trees, and Jerome sighed and winked and giggled as if the boy had miraculously named Jerome's own favorite tree. Birch was what I finally came up with, and when I told Jerome that, he looked at me.

—Birch? he said. —Them peely white things? Girl, he said, —live a little.

He, he told me grandly, would be a magnolia, as sweet as honey, with beautiful pink flowers dripping all over the ground. Mostly these are the kinds of conversations we have; they are about nothing and they go nowhere. Now and then, he asks me where my people are. No matter what I say, sooner or later he asks again.

I tell Jerome they are dead, and his eyes go wide with the pity and horror of it all.

Live girls

—Mine too, he always says, sighing dramatically, —mine too.
His parents, he tells me, died when he was young, leaving him
in the care of two evil aunts in Iowa; he is an orphan, he says, a
sad little orphan, raised by demons. It is their fault he hates
women, he explains, theirs and his mother's. His father was a
saint, he says, an African prince, tall and handsome, but his
mother was white, a monster who hated him for being a boy and
who dressed him in girls' clothes. He told me once that if he
had been raised by his father, he would have been different,
well adjusted. He'd have a good job instead of working at the
7-Eleven, and he'd have a normal family, like everyone else, a
wife, children. I asked him if he wanted a wife and children,
and he looked horrified.
—Honey, he said, —bite your tongue. He let out a little giggle.
—Me with kids, he said. —You go on. He brought his hands to
his mouth to cover his smile, but above them his eyes burned.
But what did it matter, he went on after a moment; he was an
orphan, abandoned by monsters, raised by monsters, living in
a world of monsters, an orphan, a sad dark delicate flower. He
enjoys talking about his parents' deaths; the cause was always
something violent: most of the time he says it was a plane crash
from which none of the bodies were recovered; every now and
then it was a car accident—a fiery inferno, he calls it, that mutilated their bodies beyond recognition; and once, incredibly,
they were eaten by rogue alligators at a Florida tourist park.
There was nothing left of them—nothing but their shoes and his
mother's purse. There is never anything left of them.
I imagine his parents are just like mine, sitting quietly in their
living rooms, consuming their meals, looking forward to their
television shows. I never question Jerome too closely about his
parents; once when he told me they died in a plane crash, I reminded him that only a day or so earlier it had been a car accident, and he got snippy, then left our booth and didn't talk to
me for two days. Right now, his eyes are fixed intently on a cou-

ple in the corner—a prostitute and a man she is picking up. Jerome's face is blazing with hate, and it takes me a few minutes to realize that the woman is, by some freakish chance, wearing the same shoes as Jerome—strappy bright-green heels. I can tell that he is considering some action, but just as he begins to rise, the waitress returns with our food. Jerome looks down at his wax beans.

—Excuse me, he says, —this isn't what I ordered. The waitress looks at the beans.

—It's what you ordered, she says with a practiced sigh.

Jerome looks at me. —Tell her, he says. —Tell her this isn't what I ordered.

He looks from the beans to me and back again, while the waitress stares at something across the room.

—It's what you ordered, I say, and he opens and closes his mouth once, like a colorful fish. The waitress gets away while she can, and Jerome looks down at the little chipped bowl full of yellow water and yellow beans with a few pale seeds floating on top. He sighs, then picks up his fork, and looks at my doughnut.

—I meant to order a doughnut, he says. —Or a chocolate sundae. I push my plate across the table toward him, but he shakes his head.

—Girl's got to watch her figure, he says. He stabs at the beans with his fork, spearing several of them, one after another, then brings the whole clump to his mouth. He chews slowly, and stops to breathe before he swallows, as if the whole process causes him pain. He has eaten only a few bites when he puts down his fork and watches a man and a woman come in. The man stands in the doorway, looking around; he is familiar, somehow, and it takes me a moment to recognize him as the man who was at the theater earlier with the hooker—only a few hours since I saw him and already I am having trouble placing his face. When he sees Jerome, he says something to the woman

and heads over to our booth. Jerome turns away, toward the
mirror; when the man reaches our booth, Jerome does not look
at him.

—Hey, the man says. —Hey, and finally Jerome turns; he wipes
his mouth daintily with his napkin.

—Oh, he says. —You.

—Yeah, the man says. —Me.

He glances at me. —Hey, he says. —Who's your friend?

Jerome looks at me. —That's Eric, Jerome says, waving his arm
toward the man.

—Hey, Eric says. He stares at me a moment. —Hey, he says.
—I seen you before.

I look at him. —No, I say. —I've never seen you. I'm new in
town.

—Uh-huh, he says; he nods, gazing at me. —Well, he finally
says, —I see a lot of people in my line of work. He nods, glancing around the room. —I'm a entrepreneur, he says, and
Jerome snorts delicately.

—Entrepreneur, he says, and Eric levels him a look.

—Yeh, he says. He stares at Jerome a long moment, and Jerome
looks down at his beans, the muscles in his jaw working. Eric
glances over in the corner. The woman he came with is cruising
a couple of sailors, and he says, —Hey, listen, I got to go. He
winks at me, and Jerome watches him walk away.

—That trash, Jerome says, then turns and watches in the mirror as Eric corrals the woman and leaves with her. He does
not notice when I get up to go to the bathroom, and when I
come back to our booth, he is at the counter, ostensibly ordering a cup of coffee, but as he waits, he lets his long arm drift
toward a tense, youngish man who sits on the stool next to
him; the man's eyes are closed, but his foot beats against the
rung of his stool as he waits for the touch of Jerome's hand
on his.

. . .

The streets are empty and airless as I walk home, but even so, I feel watched, tracked by the eyes of things that live in cracks, things that are caught in the space between alive and not alive. Behind me the Hygienic is just a dirty bloom of yellow on the corner; no one inside will have noticed that I am gone.

Though it is late, about half the lights in my hotel are lit, which gives it a deceptively homey, cheerful look, the look of a place where people are waiting up for someone, though most of the people inside have no one to wait up for, and are probably not even awake themselves; it's a building full of people who, for all kinds of reasons, prefer to sleep with the lights on. My own window is a square of darkness near the top. I chose this hotel because of a sign in the window that read TRANSIENTS WEL-COME; as it turned out, transients are not particularly welcome, but then neither is anyone else. I was also attracted by a ragged string of bright Christmas lights that hung haphazardly across the front of the building, though Christmas was several months past at the time. Every so often, the lights blink abruptly on for no apparent reason, and stay on for as long as two or three weeks, day and night, so that by now, even though Christmas is approaching, there is nothing really festive about them anymore.

I live on the top floor, which seems to be the least transient. My room is what is commonly described in classified ads as small but clean, and though it is certainly small, I can't imagine what it would take to make it clean. The walls are painted light green, and for furniture I have a single bed, a night table, and a chair. There is a window overlooking an alley. I do not have: a hot plate, a radio, or a pet. The man on one side of me has a radio; the man on the other side has a cat, and although hot plates are strictly forbidden, everyone but me seems to have one; the halls always smell of cooking. The smell of food lingers in the corri-dors, and creeps through the walls to settle into the plaster and wood, so that long after something has been cooked and eaten, its odor remains.

Tonight there is something sour and milky in the air, something a little rotten, and I close my door on it. I switch on my overhead light and lie down on my bed, reminding myself, as I do most nights, to go to a store tomorrow and get myself a little lamp to put by my bed, so that I do not have to get up again in order to switch off the light. The lamp I had by my bed as a child was shaped like a little sheep, with a puffy white ceramic face, and a lightbulb coming right out of the top of its head, like some sort of growth. There was something grotesque to me, even then, about the way the sheep's head sprouted that bulb, something a little unwholesome. I suppose it is still there, coated with a furry gray skin of dust, waiting next to my bed.

My sister's lamp, next to her bed, was in the shape of a pony, and its bulb came out of its back, like some sort of mutant rider, with a tiny shade on top, like a hat. She took it with her when she moved out of our room, taking herself and all of her things into a tiny closet-like space at the end of the hall. My parents called it the guest room, though we never had any guests; they continued to call it that after my sister moved into it, and I imagine they call it that still.

My sister left nothing at all in her half of our room when she moved out, not even a puff of dust. I did not know she was leaving; I came home from school one day and she was gone. The door to the guest room was closed, and I stood outside it, listening to her move things around. There was so little space inside, and I tried to imagine where she was putting her things—where her bed would go, where her head would be when she slept at night. I put my ear against the door, and she stopped, and was silent a long time; then I could feel her on the other side. I could hear her breathe. I could smell her skin through the thin wood. I put my hand against the door.

—I'm leaving you now, she whispered. —Goodbye forever.

I went back to my room and sat on my bed; even the nails that had held her pictures up had been neatly pulled from the walls. Everything that had been hers was gone, everywhere she had had something was empty. I left it that way, because I could not think of what to put in its place. I had grown so used to her and her things; her half of the room was a mirror image of my own—our parents had bought us everything the same—furniture and bedclothes and pictures and toys. For the first several years of our lives, I owned nothing that she did not have a copy of. I could look at her side of the room and see a reflection of my own. And she herself was nearly a mirror image of me; we were alike in size and hair color and eyes. All that distinguished us were the dark blistered ropes of scars that covered one side of her face, running from her forehead all the way to her chin. They were scars from a childhood accident, a steam vaporizer overturning into her crib.

I do not remember my sister's accident, though I was nearly a year older than she, and I would have been there when it happened. Sometimes I lie on my bed at night and try to remember it, but at those moments my mind goes perfectly blank, empty of thought or fact or memory; it is like a room no one has ever entered, a room without doors or windows, a place where nothing happens. To leave such scars, it must have been a terrible accident; it seems impossible to me that I do not remember it.

My parents did not ever mention my sister's accident; they did not look directly at her face; they seldom addressed her at all. And, in what I suppose was some misguided effort at equal treatment, they likewise averted their eyes from my own face. Even when they addressed us directly, they looked away—to the side, or down, or over our heads, so consistently looking away from us that I sometimes wondered, if something happened to us and our parents were called upon to identify the bodies, whether they could have done so, so unaccustomed were they to looking at our faces. Occasionally my mother did shift her eyes from my father to me, and then I would look up to find her watching me with a kind of blank speculative gaze. It always made me feel that there was something I was supposed to be doing, something other than whatever it was I was doing at the time. Whenever she addressed my sister, she looked at me.

My sister had as little interest in our parents as they in her, but me she hated. I was, in her eyes, undamaged, and as such, all the things she wanted—boys, friends, love—were available to me. And, in fact, I suppose they were, and that I had none of them seemed to infuriate her as she sat by and watched me squander all I did not deserve to possess.

We did not have conversations: when she talked to me, it was angry short bursts, and when she looked at me it was to stare at me when she thought I could not see her, or to watch me from around corners at school; at home, she sat in a puddle of darkness on her bed, her face turned away from the light.

She spent most of her time reading magazines. She surrounded herself with pictures she tore from them and tacked up on the walls, pictures of beautiful women gazing down at her, and she sat among them, waiting to be saved. She believed that boys climbed at night in the trees outside her window, peeking in to watch her, and that sooner or later one of them would be brave enough to tap at the glass and carry her away. She would leave me forever, and I would be left all alone, she told me. No one would ever love me. She spent whole evenings sitting at our bedroom window, gazing out, waiting. I sat on my bed and watched her, and after she moved out of our room, I used to go outside and sit on the lawn below, looking up at her. She sat at her window, unmoving, her face covered with our mother's old wedding veil, which she had found in our attic.

I close my eyes. The overhead light is harsh, despite the saucer of glass that covers the bulb, and the light it casts is mottled with the splotchy corpses of flies and insects that have been trapped inside. Soon, when it is quieter, I will get up and turn off the light, though it is never really quiet here. There is always someone moving, or talking, or doing something; even up here, where there are only a handful of us, it is never quiet.

My neighbor to the left is the loudest; he keeps his radio on almost all the time, even when he is not in, and he keeps it tuned to a station that broadcasts only sports—"All sports, all the time," vows its cheerless jingle, which is followed by the crack of a bat, then the surging roar of a crowd. Usually it is people calling in, asking questions or offering opinions, and most of the callers seem to be drunk or irate or both, and what most of them want is for someone—a manager, a coach, a player, it hardly seems to matter—to be fired. My neighbor is not an athletic-looking man; he's pale and puffy and walks with a hitch. It's hard to imagine him playing a sport.

On my other side is the man with the cat, though pets are not allowed in the building. We had a pet only briefly when I was growing up, a big black cat who showed up in the driveway one night. For some reason my parents allowed me to bring him in. He was patient and tolerant, but he never seemed very comfortable with us, no matter how hard I tried to make him feel at home. I carried him every night into our room, and placed him gently at the foot of my bed, where he would glance quickly from my sister to me, then suddenly begin to clean himself wherever I had touched him. My sister pretended to have no interest in him, but I could see her watching him in the mirror as he washed himself. When he jumped down from my bed and went to wait at the door to be let out, as he always did, she would turn and smile.

—See? she'd say. —He doesn't want to be *your* pet.

Every morning when I woke up, he was still sitting at the door, as though he had sat there waiting all night, but there were times I woke up and I could have sworn he was at the foot of my bed; I could hear his tiny breath; I could move my feet and feel something solid. It's hard to believe I could have imagined such a thing, something so real as that.

I could tell the cat made my parents nervous, sitting in the corner, watching us as we watched television, and we had him only a few weeks before he disappeared. My mother told me that my father had taken him to a farm to live, where he could roam, though they knew no one with a farm. They knew no one at all, really, and when my sister and I were not at school, our lives were spent only in the company of one another, which was hardly anything that could be called company, more like a random grouping of humans thrown together as part of an experiment, instructed to go on with our lives as if we were alone. The cat was a welcome relief.

His name was probably Blackie, or Midnight, some dark name, and for a year or two after he disappeared, I waited for him to return; sometimes I watched for him in the woods at the edge of our housing development, and I was sure I saw him, a black shadow under a tree, gazing down at the bright warm lights of all our houses.

The cat next door is named Debbie and her owner talks to her all the time; sometimes it sounds like he has a friend in there with him he is so chatty and conversational, but most of the time he speaks to her in a dreamy slow murmur. Some mornings when I lie awake in the very early day, all I can hear is her name, over and over, like words said in a trance. I see her often; her owner leaves his door ajar whenever he goes to the bathroom down the hall. She is a skinny black-and-orange thing, with pale-yellow eyes. Lately, every time I see her, she is hunched motionless with her head hung down over a large pink bowl of water. I can see by her eyes and her greasy fur that she is sick, and once I tried mentioning this to her owner. Didn't I have any business of my own to mind? was his response, and now when we pass in the hallway, he refuses to meet my eyes, and if I pause to speak, he begins to cough and does not stop until he's back in the room with Debbie, the door locked safely behind him.

Debbie herself makes no noise at all, which is, I suppose, why she has not been found out. Sometimes I think I hear a meow and I am quiet to listen, but it always turns out to be a pigeon or some animal in the alley.

Tonight there are the usual noises around me—the radio, the noise of feet on the stairs, the opening and closing of doors, the flush of water. Finally, I rise to turn off my light. I would like to say that I fall then into a deep and dreamless sleep, but instead I lie stiffly on top of my stiff blanket, waiting for the objects in my room to reshape themselves in the dark.

Sleep here is nothing like rest, but rather a dead stop to thought, and we all stir uneasily all night, lying only a wall on either side away from people who are strangers to us.

Somewhere my sister and I were taught a prayer; *And if I die before I wake* went one of its lines, which my sister, on the rare occasions she prayed, changed to *Let me die before I wake.* Then she'd lean into the dark chasm between us. Tonight's the night, she'd say, I can feel it. Goodbye, she'd intone, Goodbye forever, and then she would lie on her back, her arms crossed on her chest, to be ready, she said, for the undertaker. Then she'd open her eyes. Be sure it's a closed coffin, she always added. I don't want them looking at me.

No one looked at her when she died. The coffin was closed, and there was no one there but the three of us.

—Debbie, croons the man next door. —Debbie, he repeats, his voice rising, falling, and I turn onto my stomach and wonder what it would be like to be the object of such pure, focused attention. I think of him lying on the floor next to Debbie as she hangs her head over her bowl. He whispers her name and stares at her beautiful yellow eyes, her soft ears, her shining fur. He cannot see that she is dying.

Live girls

By now Dave must be home, lying next to his wife in their bed. He will lie awake a long time, his eyes wide open, unable to sleep. He is thinking about Art, and how one day it will save him. Beside him his wife dozes uneasily, never really sleeping. Jolted awake at the touch of Dave's hands on her throat, she looks at him; he is so still beside her and she gazes at him a long while, watching his chest rise, fall, rise, trying to read in its rhythm if he is only feigning sleep. His hands are hidden under the blankets. Was he touching her? She cannot tell. Finally, she closes her eyes again, and sleeps or does not sleep; she can hardly tell any longer what it is to be asleep or awake, and she drifts a bit, only to be roused again by something beside her—a breath, a murmur, a slight shift of the body. It is so hard for her to sleep, and there are so many things to fear. I wonder suddenly if Danny is her nephew or the nephew of Dave's first wife, the wife he killed. I wonder what Danny thought as he gazed across the street at me, lit up in my ticket bubble, and if he is thinking of me now, already dreaming of our life together. I wonder if my sister thought of me before she died, or if her thoughts were only of herself, and of whatever boy would come for her, his face hidden in the dark leaves outside her window. I wonder what her face looked like when she died, and if she thought of me then.

I turn on my side, close my eyes, open them, and wait for my mind to empty into sleep. All around me is the uneasy hum of humanity running like a current from room to room as we all lie on our beds trying not to think of our options. In every corner lurks the shadow of disappointment, waiting to creep in and attach itself to me, to move as I move, to turn as I turn, like a tin can tied to the tail of a dog, giving off the noisy rattle of expectation.

I wake to the flush of the toilet in the bathroom at the end of the hall. There is a single bathroom for all of us on this floor. The man to my right seems to use it the most; he takes long baths, sometimes two or three times a day, sometimes for as long as an hour. He seems always to be heading for the bathroom or returning from it, dressed in his ratty orange terry-cloth robe, carrying a stack of magazines, a bar of soap hanging from his neck on a rope; the soap is always in the shape of something—a frog, a boat, a fish—though after a few days of use it dissolves into a shapeless lump. Last week when we passed in the hallway, he had a new soap hanging down in the V of his robe; I stared at it the whole time it took us to pass, trying to figure out what it was, but only after he had shut his door behind him did I realize it was a penis; it was the color that threw me, a light bluish-green.

He always leaves the bathroom wet, smelling of something creepy and sweet. Not long ago, I used it after him and found his stack of magazines left in a damp pile next to the tub, the covers puckered with steam. The magazine on top featured a blond woman, naked but for what looked like a leather harness and a pair of handcuffs, which locked her arms to a metal pole behind her. Her mouth was a red circle, her eyes closed, her head thrown back in the usual pose. I left the magazines where they were, and when I came out of the bathroom, my neighbor was waiting outside his door, pacing back and forth in an agitated little shuffle, his hair still sticking up in wet tufts. He passed me without a glance, and when he came back out of the bathroom, his magazines pressed jealously against his chest, he gave me a quick vicious glance before he went back into his own room. I noticed that day that he had slippers that matched his robe, orange terry-cloth, and flat, with no backs, so that they flapped against his heels as he walked.

Someone is walking past my door, and I try to guess who it is, what face goes with the footsteps; I should recognize them all by now, but it is nothing more than the comings and goings of strangers. I close my eyes; it feels as if my life has been spent tracking the comings and goings of strangers. My mother, my father, my sister, all strangers. My heart moves, a weak muscle fluttering in my chest.

When the hall is still, I get up and take my little toilet bag into the bathroom. The mirror is fogged over, and the sink ringed with a grimy circle of shaved hair. To wash my face I have to straddle a puddle of water in front of the sink. I am not used to sharing a bathroom with men and the things they leave behind them. We had our own bathroom, my sister and I, just off our bedroom. In the several months before she moved out of our room entirely, she took to spending nights there. She had to, she said; she had to get away from me. She claimed I watched her in her bed at night, waiting for her to fall asleep. She was afraid of me, and it was my fault she never slept, she told me; if it had not been for me, everything would have been different. I shared a bathroom again at the college, with all the girls on my floor, who stood every morning in front of the mirror, gazing serenely at their round pleasant faces. I always stood a little apart, watching them clean themselves, face after face after face, all cleaning themselves for God. When they finished, they left no traces of themselves; where there had been a row of clean, shining girls was now a row of clean, shining sinks, and I took my place at one of them. I never felt comfortable with them in the room; their eyes seemed always to be meeting in the glass around me or behind me or over my head, a conspiracy of glances, and I would bend over my toilet bag, rooting around in it as though I were searching for something, until they left.

I still have the bag, a pink plastic thing printed with little animals walking through a rainstorm, each carrying a tiny umbrella. My mother bought it for me before I left to come here; it's full of whimsy, something she lacks entirely, and I can't imagine what possessed her to buy it, except that perhaps, as she stood there looking over the display, she saw herself standing in a long line of girls, her little bag on the sink in front, and in the mirror her own face—young, and with nothing to think of but herself. All of us—me, my sister, even my father—would be nothing but ideas, vague plans for the future. She left the bag for me in my room, and when my sister saw it, she snatched it from my bed, examined it, then tossed it back.

—That'll be a big hit, she said. —You'll be the star of the bathroom.

As I return to my room, Debbie's owner is leaving his; he stands at his door, looking in, and as I pass, I glance inside to see Debbie, crouched at her bowl, her head hanging down. Her owner is murmuring something to her, words I can't catch; he doesn't look at me as I pass, but his back stiffens and he waits until I've opened my own door before he closes the door to his and walks away. I listen to his footsteps down the stairs; then I come back out into the hallway and go to his door.

—Debbie, I whisper. Even with my ear to the door there is no sound. I pat the door, then go back to my room. I would like to have a little cat waiting there for me to return: it would look up when I entered, it would listen to the things I said. I sit at the chair by my window, overlooking the alley below, and think of the things I would like to have, the things I want. Cat, I think.

Live girls

I write it down: *Cat*. Here I run out of ideas; there are things I want; I know there are things I want, but it is not yet clear to me what they are. *Hot plate*, I write; *radio*. The television shows my parents watched were full of people who wanted things; that's all there was, was wanting. I try to remember some of the things they wanted. *Television*, I add to my list.

Outside, in the alley, a commotion rises. I look out to see two women arguing over a chair by a Dumpster. One is sitting in the chair, holding tightly to the arms, while the other tugs at it, dragging it in little hops along the ground. It's an easy chair, with a blue-and-white pattern. I add it to my list. It would go nicely in the corner, and in the evenings I would sit there, my cat dozing on my feet. We would cook our dinner on our hot plate while we listened to our radio and watched our television. Together we would spend our lives here. We would never have to leave our room. In the alley, the woman pulling on the chair gives up; she turns to walk off, saying something over her shoulder to the woman behind her, who watches her walk away, then stays sitting in the chair. She looks bewildered, as if she does not know what to do now that she has won. I close my eyes. Cat, I think. Hot plate. Radio.

When I open my eyes again, the woman is gone from the alley; she has left the chair where it was, beside the Dumpster. Yellow foam blooms from a hole in the middle of the seat. I rise and head downstairs. Today is rent day. Except for the bottom floor, where the rooms go by the day, the rooms here rent by the week. Not a long time, but even so, there are regular purges–people hustled out, their suitcases split open on the sidewalk, radios smashed on the pavement next to them. To keep us honest, the back doors are sealed up, there are no fire escapes, and all the lower windows are barred. The only way out is through the grimy lobby and past the manager, who sits in a little cage near the front door. He collects the rent and cleans the bathrooms. These seem to be his only duties; nothing else here is attended to: blown bulbs remain dark, windows that were cracked when I arrived are still unreplaced, and every corner is padded with thick little cushions of dust. The manager spends all his time in his cage; he is a skinny, squirrely man, all long bones, with long bony ears, a long thin nose, and long sparse hairs trailing over his bony spotted scalp. Everything about him is long and unhealthy-looking, bloodless and pale, like some rootbound plant kept in a basement so long it's turned white as it stretches blindly across the floor in search of light.

I have never heard the manager addressed by name; no one talks to him and he talks to no one. He seems possessed of a violent hatred for his job, and he makes it clear that what he hates most about it is us, whom he watches come and go with weary loathing, as if we are a colony of insects he has spent a lifetime trying to eradicate. He sits in his cage like a spider, gathering his strength for the distasteful task of taking our money, a chore he performs without looking at or talking to or touching any of us. It's hard to consider what life he might have outside his cage, but, in fact, he has a little room of his own off the lobby, which he shares with his wife. She is unbalanced, and spends most of her time lurking in the alley beside the building, but she is, nonetheless, his wife, and living testimony that there was at least one moment in his life when he was willing to endure the company of another person.

He is staring down at a newspaper when I stop at his cage to pay; I stand in front of him a moment, but he doesn't look up, and finally I slide my money through the slot at the bottom of the cage. He looks at it over the paper, then takes it by the corner and deposits it in a little box. Usually he checks off my room number, but today he just goes back to his paper.

—That's room twelve, I say, and wait a beat, but he says nothing.

—In case you want to write it down, I add. He looks up at me, his gaze stopping somewhere at the level of my chin.

—You know, I say. —In case you don't remember it.

—I can remember it, he says, and goes back to the paper, staring down at the sports section. It surprises me that he follows sports; it would surprise me to see that he took an actual interest in anything, and I bend my head to see what he is reading. He looks up again, this time raising his eyes as far as my nose.

—What? he asks testily.

—The bathroom on five, I say. —It smells kind of strange— which is true enough, but it always smells strange, and the manager lowers his paper.

—The bathroom smells kind of strange, he repeats tonelessly and for just a moment it seems he might actually take this comment seriously. I nod, and he shakes his head, then hazards a look at my forehead, which he stares at for a while before his face explodes into a sudden sour fury.

—I cleaned the bathroom Monday, he says, leaning forward. The paper flutters to the floor, and he looks at it a moment, then back at me, enraged. —I clean the fucking bathroom every Monday. Every fucking Monday.

He bends to snatch up his paper, then scrapes his chair along the floor so that he is turned sideways, his body facing away from mine. He rattles his paper open in front of him.

—The bathroom smells kind of strange, he mutters, letting out a noise that could very well be a laugh. His long fingers tremble against the paper like uncontrollable little children as he allows himself this moment of amusement. This is the longest conversation we have ever had.

Outside, it is warm and bright, and I have hours to kill. Sometimes I walk over to a nearby park, full of pigeons and squirrels and people Dave refers to as nuts. You want to watch out for those nuts, he always tells me, you never know what those nuts are capable of. And some of them are nuts, but all they seem capable of is sitting on benches all day long, and keeping up a non-stop patter of psychosis, a muttered litany of remembered injuries, imagined injuries, anticipated injuries. They stare you right in the face when you walk by them. Most of the benches, though, are occupied by people who are not nuts, but who simply have nowhere else to go, no one else to talk to, and nothing else to do besides sit on a bench staring numbly at whatever passes by. Some days I am one of them.

Down the street, coming from the direction of the park, is Ned, one of the roomers on my floor. He is an old queen of sixty or so, who spends most of his time on the phone on the landing, talking to his mother, who lives in a nursing home nearby. Sometimes when I leave my room, I hear him talking to her, and I stop and sit on the steps to listen, just out of his sight, eavesdropping on the weary promises he makes to her daily, promises he cannot possibly keep: she will feel better tomorrow; one day soon he will get a little house and she will come to live there with him; he will not let her die all alone in her room, surrounded by strangers; he will not let her die. —Mother, he sighs into the phone, —Mother, I promise. His reedy voice is weary with the constant reassurance. If I pass him while he is on the phone, he turns away from me to the wall, and puts his arm up, as if he is guarding something. After a while on the phone with his mother, his eyes are like little blue marbles. He leaves the bathroom very clean.

Whenever we pass, Ned moves away from me, and will never meet my eyes; as he approaches the building now, he cuts a wide circle around me. I step away from the door toward him, and he jigs suddenly out into the street, not even pretending it is for any reason other than to avoid me. Once inside, he will make a formal, precise ceremony of paying his rent, laying out each bill neatly, counting as he does so, then insisting on a receipt. I've watched him go through the process a few times.

I admire his persistence; while the manager glares hatefully at him, his hands trembling with outrage at the request, Ned stares at the wall, waiting for the receipt. Finally, the manager scrawls it out on a scrap of paper and thrusts it at him. He must have hundreds of them by now; I imagine he saves them as carefully as he acquires them, storing them in a shoebox under his bed, bringing them out perhaps only to display to his mother, to show her the life he has been reduced to while she bleeds away all the money that he has, dying in her home.

He pats his pinkish hair now, as he waits for his receipt. It's done up in stiff pompadour, bizarrely debonair, and while I imagine it deeply impresses the nurses at his mother's home, it probably does not go over well in the bars, where the men who look like Ned are always the ones standing unwatched in corners, or perching self-consciously on bar stools, smiling uselessly out at a crowd of beautiful men, their hands gone numb from holding on so tightly to their cold drinks.

When the manager at last shoves Ned's receipt at him, and Ned bends his head to examine it, I head for the Hygienic.

During the day, it is a different place. Light bleaches out the splotches of black on the mirrors, and even if it did not, during the day it is full of people who would never think to look in a mirror. There are cops, and a few people like me, but mostly there are old men, who come here because they have no place else to go. They all seem, more or less, to know each other, and they spend their time discussing whatever gruesome crime is most recently in the news. Anything local is best—the occasional prostitute-killing occupies them for weeks—but really they are drawn to whatever is tragic anywhere: disappearances of young girls, rapes, murders, serial killings, all of which they discuss in complex, argumentative detail, as if they were talking about a sporting event. The more brutal the crime, the more acute their interest and the livelier their debate. They always discuss their crimes from the point of view of the perpetrator—why he did it, how he did it, if he'll do it again.

Lately they have been chewing over a mutilation case in Maine, which, being in the same general area of the country, makes it a semi-local crime: a woman was kidnapped from a parking lot, raped, then carved up and left on a suburban front lawn, propped up against the birdbath, like a lawn ornament. Her breasts were removed from her body. The men have been speculating for days about whether the killer was the woman's husband or a stranger committing a random act of violence; about three-quarters go with the husband, the rest a stranger, but all of them think the woman had no business being out by herself after dark. They have all agreed on this since the murder, but it's what they come back to again and again.

Dave's wife's death would have kept them occupied for weeks, trying to decide whether or not he did it on purpose.

There are no accidents, one of them would have surely said. Ain't that right? he would have appealed to one of the cops, and the cop would have puffed up with importance and nodded sagely. Cops do not believe in accidents.

When I arrive at the Hygienic, two cops are at the counter, sitting in front of huge platters of waffles; they are surrounded by a ring of old men. One of the cops is talking, but pauses to watch me walk to my booth. The other cop watches me too, as he chews. I am the only woman in here besides the waitress. The second cop swallows, then goes back to his food. I can smell the maple syrup on his waffles.

—Anyways, the first cop says, turning back to the old men, —you've got to understand, these guys don't know what else to do with women.

The other cop nods seriously, swallows, takes another bite.

—Yep, the cop goes on. —They always cut up the breasts.

He pauses, and holds his cup up for the waitress to refill.

—And the face, he adds. He glances around the room and catches me watching him, then smiles pleasantly, as if he is explaining how he fixed the leak in his sink.

—Yeah, so like I was saying, he says, shifting his eyes back to the men, —breasts, face, they're always the first to get cut up.

The old man nearest him rattles his cup into his saucer, quivering with excitement. His eyes glisten.

Another clump of cops comes in, and the waitress brings me the pancakes I have ordered; they are gummy at the center when I cut into them, and I push my plate away and drink the rest of my coffee.

The new cops settle in at the counter with the cops who were already there, and the old men turn to each other, speculating on the significance of the yard where the woman's body was left. They wonder if perhaps the family who owned it might be involved, and what might be the significance of the birdbath. Things like this did not happen where I grew up. Or if they did, we did not hear about them. My parents did not have friends, and my sister and I did not have friends; we talked to no one, and played alone behind the tall fence my parents put up around our yard. We could hear neighbors through the fence, sometimes catch glimpses of them through the wooden slats. On one side was a family with children and several pets, and when my sister was very young, she used to spend hours huddled against the side of the fence that bordered their yard; she would stare at them through the slats, then start digging little holes at the base of the fence. She would dig furiously, then stop, look up and stare at me, sitting several yards away watching her, then go back to digging, piling the dirt up in little mounds at her side. My mother hovered at the kitchen window all day watching us, finally bringing us in at dusk. When we went out the next morning, my sister's holes were always neatly filled in, the dirt patted firmly down; she would stare at them a moment, then set to digging anew. As we grew older, she lost interest in the neighbors and in digging, and after a while she stopped going outside altogether, but even when I left, years later, grass had still not grown along the fence where she used to sit: a strip of dirt ran like a scar along its base. When I left, she sat at her window and watched me go. Or she did not. There was something at her window, something dark, hovering at the glass, but it could have been nothing more than a shadow cast by someone on the other side of the room.

As I leave the Hygienic, the old men are debating what the killer did with the woman's breasts, which have not been recovered; they are wondering what someone would do with a pair of breasts, how you would keep them, what they would look and feel like. A few of the cops watch me walk out, chewing as their eyes drop to check out my body.

The theater is open when I arrive; my bubble is already lit up, and the doors are unlocked. Dave is seldom here so early; it is my job to open the theater, to turn on the lights, to get it ready for the evening. He comes around the counter when I enter; the smell of burnt popcorn is already in the air, but before I mention it to Dave, he nods at the other end of the room. Sitting there, on the green plastic couch that no one ever uses, is the boy from the bench across the street last night. He is staring earnestly at the floor. A little bag of popcorn sits on his lap. Behind the couch stand two large cardboard prop-ups of women dressed in leather underwear, their breasts on either side of his head.

—Danny, Dave barks, and the boy stands abruptly, sending a shower of popcorn to the floor. He looks down at it in dismay, then back up at us.

—My wife's sister's kid, Dave says to me, waving in the general direction of the boy. —Danny.

Danny crosses the room to us and holds out his hand, which is soft, and slightly oily from the popcorn. He is tall and pale and a little doughy, with an odd haircut, longish but layered, with bangs and puffed up from the crown like the crest of a bird.

—She's a college girl, Dave announces, as though he himself has been responsible for educating me.

—I know, Danny says. He looks down at the floor.

—I was planning on going to college, he adds after a moment, and Dave rolls his eyes.

—I know, Dave says. —That's why I'm introducing you. He looks at me. —You two will have a lot in common, he explains. It's clear that Danny has prepared for this night; his skin is still pink from shaving, and his nails are so clean and freshly cut that the skin around them is still red and the little white moon at the base of each nail gleams in the light. Even his jeans are pressed, with sharp creases running slightly off center down the front of each leg. He is probably the kind of boy my mother thinks I am meeting at the places she thinks I am going; he is probably the kind of boy she imagined she herself would meet at those places, the kind of boy she thinks might still be waiting for her there. He is the kind of shy polite boy my sister would have been merciless with; she would have made fun of his hair, his soft oily hands, his large round face. She would take one look at him fumbling to shake my father's hand, then glance at me and shake her head; it would confirm everything she already knew about me, everything she had spent her lifetime telling me.

He is the not the kind of boy she wanted for herself. The boys she wanted for herself were the kind of boys who hide in trees, or wait at the end of alleys, or follow you down the street. They were the kind of boys who did not care what she looked like because they did not look at her. I used to watch them watch her. Before she stopped going out entirely, I followed her sometimes, hanging back as she would slow to pass some group of boys; the boys would watch her pass, and then behind her back their eyes would meet, until after a few moments one of them peeled himself away and sauntered after her.

They never noticed me; I crossed the street, or lingered by a car until they wandered off, and then I would follow the boy who had followed my sister, to find them in some alley, pressed against a wall or the side of a house. Her head was always turned away and her hands were always on either side of her, flat against the wall behind her, while the boy ran his hands over her body, but kept his eyes turned away from her face. I watched from behind a car, or around a corner. Later at night, I'd listen to her quick breath from somewhere in the room and wonder what she was thinking when that boy was with her, and what it must have been like for him to touch her like that, to run his hands over her body, to touch her and never to look at her face.

Danny is not that kind of boy. He is the kind of boy around whom we would all feel safe. He would never follow a girl like my sister; he would never stand with a group of men and let his eyes meet theirs as a woman passed; he would never murder his wife.

—Dave's told me all about you, I tell him, which elicits a sick half-smile.

—Oh, he says, dropping my hand.

—But not very much, I say. —He didn't really tell me very much at all. I give him an encouraging nod, but he drops his head. Bits of popcorn have stuck to his jeans, and as he stares down, he slaps at himself suddenly where they have stuck, as if a swarm of mosquitoes has landed on him.

Dave shifts impatiently; he would reach out and smash us together if he could, and just be done with it. His face is full of a kind of dark anger, the intensity of which surprises me, and I smile brightly at Danny.

—Well, I say, —time to get back to work.

—Okay, Danny says with relief, and turns abruptly, heading back for the couch.

—Jesus, Dave says to him, or me, or both of us. —Jesus Christ. He shuffles off in disgust, slamming his office door behind him, then opening it immediately to look out at us, separated by the width of the lobby.

Live girls

Danny eats what's left of his popcorn as he watches me prepare the register for the night's business; this involves nothing really beyond turning it on and inserting the cash drawer, but I try to make it look complicated, frowning down at it, flipping through the bills in the drawer, nodding every now and then, and looking thoughtfully out at the passing parade of lowlife. I am trying to think of some tactful way to find out which of Dave's wives Danny belongs to—the current one, or the one he killed—it might give me a better sense of how much he expects of me, or of what Danny might feel Dave owes him—what sort of debt for which I might be partial payment.

As customers begin to wander in, Danny sits up straight and watches them, turning his head to follow them from the entrance into the theater, as if they are a parade of animals at the circus; he chews on his popcorn, as though they cannot see his head swivel to follow them.

After they've gone inside and the first show has begun, he makes his way across the lobby toward me, stopping to examine with an exaggerated nonchalance the posters Dave's put up on the wall, most of them breasts and mouths and legs; he lingers at the last one before the counter—a woman dressed all in leather, holding a whip. I can see his eyes moving sideways from the picture to me and back, and after a moment more, he pulls himself away and comes to the counter, still holding his popcorn bag. He has worried the top of it away, and crumpled the bottom, but I take it and fill it; he watches with admiration as I squirt it with fake butter, but when I hand him the bag, he drops his eyes quickly and takes his popcorn back to the couch, this time passing the posters without a look. After he is settled, I lean back to read a magazine, but I can feel his eyes on me. When I look up and catch him watching, his eyes dart away, to fix desperately on some spot on the wall that isn't me. We pass the time this way for a while, and Dave leans back in his chair, watching us through the crack in his door. This is not how he had imagined it; this is not what is supposed to happen, how he had imagined we would behave. We should have fallen in love already; we should have planned to marry within the month; it would be out of his hands then, what happened to me after that. This is how it is supposed to happen.

At the end of the first show, he comes out and stands behind me while I take tickets. I can feel his breath on my neck, but when I turn, he is staring at Danny, whose gaze is riveted on the floor a few feet in front of his shoes.

—What a moron, Dave says. —What a total fucking idiot moron. He shakes his head and goes upstairs to start the movie; Danny looks up and watches Dave as he disappears on the stairs.

The evening passes, and Danny comes back several times for popcorn; when his bag is transparent with grease, I replace it. On the third or fourth trip, he says shyly that he hopes I don't mind him eating so much popcorn. I tell him, no, we don't sell much of it. I consider telling him that Dave eats most of it anyways, but I decide against it, and wait for him to hand me his bag and let me fill it and then make the return trip back to his couch. Instead, he stands in front of me, looking a little dazed. I can tell he is searching for a conversation starter. His glance falls to my magazine. One of the cover lines is something about Washington, D.C., and Danny muses over it a moment, then looks nonchalantly out the window; he pops a piece of popcorn into his mouth, then asks me, as though the thought has come to him out of nowhere, if I have ever been to our nation's capital. I tell him yes; and he gazes at me, waiting. —In seventh grade, I add, —for the spelling bee. His eyes widen.

—Wow, he says, looking at me with sudden respect.

In fact, I have never been to Washington, though, like every other child in my school, I participated in our yearly spelling bees. The girl who always won was an oddly calm girl named Ramona, with red hair and thick, dry skin. Every year, we filed into the auditorium to watch her beat the rest of the children in the school, even those from higher grades, and as words I'd never heard were thrown at her, she caught them like flies buzzing around her head. —Ramification, she'd repeat, as if it were a word all fourth-graders used; —remonstrate, ideologue. She did, in fact, go to Washington, in the sixth or seventh grade, and met with miserable defeat, misspelling "fluctuate" in the first round. I looked it up the day our teacher told us this, and tried to use it on my sister, but since by then she had stopped responding to me, instead speaking to me only when she felt the urge, she just looked at me and rolled her eyes, but all that week she called me Ramona, the spelling queen. When Ramona returned, we were all ashamed of her defeat, no one more than she herself; she had had no friends, really, before her defeat, though she did have that kind of respect children offer to those who are able to do something well, but after her defeat in Washington, she lost even that, and in all subsequent spelling bees she would misspell the first word she was given, then sit at her desk and gaze vaguely out the window.

I tell Danny I won the spelling bee in Washington, and he shakes his head, awed. I tell him I met the vice president.
—Wow, he says again. —What was your word?
—Fluctuate, I say, and his face goes so red it is clear he thinks the word means something sexual, something like "fuck," but because I don't really know how to reassure him without actually saying "fuck," I just smile and say it again softly, then spell it out. He bends the rim of his popcorn bag until he recovers enough from his embarrassment to ask me what my favorite color is.

Somewhere I have read that blue is the usual answer, but even as I think of the word, I cannot remember for a moment what blue is, what it looks like. I close my eyes and think of blue, but all I can see is yellow: yellow sun, yellow sky, yellow fields full of yellow flowers—a world of yellow, and not a single shadow. I would live there if I could.

—Blue, I say. Danny smiles shyly; after a moment I realize he is wearing a blue shirt.

—Me too, he says, and looks down at his mutilated bag. I reach for it, and he looks up, startled, until he realizes what I am reaching for; he stares at my hand a moment, then releases the bag.

When I turn back to him, he seems to have planted himself firmly; his feet are rooted solidly into the carpet, his hands spread on the counter. I put the popcorn on the glass between his hands and he stares down at it.

—So, he says, then stops abruptly; his eyes flicker around the lobby as he waits for conversation. I start to turn away.

—Soooo, he says again, then sighs. I glance at Dave's office and catch him watching us through the crack in his door, leaning precariously sideways in his chair to hear us. Our eyes meet, and he shifts them quickly to the floor, but stays in his awkward position, as if his body just naturally found its way into such discomfort. Danny's eyes follow my gaze, and both of us stare at Dave; when I look away, I can hear the sigh of his chair as he eases it down. Danny keeps his eyes on Dave, and plunges his hand into his popcorn, then puts a fistful of it into his mouth.

—So, I say. —Dave says you work for the city.

He looks at me, alarmed; his mouth is still full of popcorn. He stops chewing, then swallows whole what is left in his mouth. His throat throbs with the effort.

—Yes, he finally says, and nods several times, but offers nothing more, still swallowing. I consider what exactly it might mean to work for the city. Cops work for the city, and garbage collectors, and meter readers; looking at Danny, it is not hard to imagine him walking from house to house in a neat blue uniform, keeping earnest track of people's energy usage.

I lean forward on my elbows toward him; this is the kind of thing I used to find in the magazines my sister read: tips on how to talk to boys, how to make them more at ease, how to make them like you. Leaning forward was always first or second on such lists, before or after smiling and not talking about oneself. It doesn't seem to be working with Danny, who takes a step backward and looks nervously toward Dave's office. Sometimes at night my sister used to practice some of the things she read about in her magazines; she sat at our little vanity table and leaned on her elbows, ducked her head shyly, smiled over her shoulder, tossed her hair, practicing for encounters she would never have; then she would see me watching her in the mirror and turn and stare at me a long moment in the dark, until I had to close my eyes and turn away.

This is the first time I have ever actually tried anything like this; I did not talk much to boys in school. I did not talk much to anyone in school. Although I was older, our birth dates put my sister and me in the same grade, and for our first years of school she was always with me, cleaved to my side like an extra limb. When I turned, she turned, when I moved, she moved, when I breathed, she breathed; she was always there; she was always beside me.

The other children stared at her, though the teachers tried to train them not to, their eyes focused like little black circles on her face, and, so close beside hers, on mine. I must have seemed as much a curiosity to them as my sister. Every now and then, I saw a teacher pull aside a small staring boy or girl, then bend to give a whispered lecture while the child's face went cloudy with resentment. The lectures did no good, of course, and under the pressure of those staring eyes, my sister turned her face to me. All the other children turned their faces to her, and she turned hers to me, and I turned mine away. I studied posters and windows and walls, and when I could, I began to edge away from her; I put an inch between us, and then a foot, and then a yard.

At first she struggled along at my heels, then gradually fell away—but she was always there, always somewhere, standing by a drinking fountain, her eyes on me, or lurking at the end of the hall, her face just visible from behind a row of lockers.

As we all grew older, the other children got used to my sister, and though none of them became her friends, they absorbed her into the fabric that makes up the background of a childhood; by now her face is just another detail in an imperfect memory. Oh yes, one of them might be saying even now, there was this terribly scarred little girl–all the other children were so cruel to her, but I always tried to be kind.

She would become another way for them to refigure their own roles in their own histories, while me they would forget, except perhaps as a faint memory of denser air at my sister's side, a shadow she cast as she tried to become one of them. I do not remember the faces of anyone from my school, not a teacher, not a friend; I remember only her face, always turned to me, even when she was no longer there.

Danny smiles helplessly at me as he chews his popcorn; Dave has twisted around to watch us again, and I lean a little closer.

—So, I say. —You work for the city. He stops chewing to nod, then waits a moment before he swallows, and I try again to imagine him in various kinds of city employment, but still nothing fits, so I nod and say, —That must be nice, and he nods, and together we nod until finally I ask what exactly it is he does. He sighs.

—Animal control, he answers, and then, after a moment's consideration, —Pest control.

—You're a dogcatcher? I ask, and he looks horrified.

—Oh no, he says. —Nothing like that. I couldn't do anything like that.

I say nothing, he says nothing, Dave creaks in his chair; we are all waiting.

Finally, Danny sighs again. —You know pigeons? he says, and I nod. —Well, you know how they roost all over the place? I nod again. —Well, we control them.

He puts a single piece of popcorn in his mouth and smiles weakly, apparently ending our conversation. Dave shifts uneasily at the silence between us.

—Control them? I finally say.

—Well, he says. —You know how they always roost in those underpasses? And again I nod.

—Well, he says, —we keep them from doing that.

—Oh, I say; then, —How?

He chews thoughtfully, looking out the window. —You know, he says, —we just block off the openings. With screens. Then they can't get back in.

He sighs and looks at Dave, then goes on abruptly, as if he has resigned himself to telling me everything. —Sometimes we have to gas them, he says, —if they get caught inside.

He looks at me. —They can get trapped.

He sighs and looks down at his popcorn, then rearranges a few pieces on top as if he is looking for something he's lost.

—It's a new program, he says suddenly, looking up. —We're very optimistic about it.

—It seems a little extreme, I say, and he looks at me, confused.

—For the pigeons, I add.

He appears to consider this seriously, gazing down at the candy through the glass.

—They're a nuisance, he says finally. —A public nuisance. He sighs. —Don't you think?

—I don't know, I say. I wipe the counter off with a napkin, though it is already clean but for a little greasy blot of warmth where I set Danny's most recent bag of popcorn.

—It's a city program, Danny says. —The people want it. I wouldn't do it if the people didn't want it.

—Oh, I say, —a city program.

Danny's face floods with relief.

—Yeah, he says. —A city program. It's new.

He nods, then I nod; and for a moment we stand there nodding. Dave leans sideways to watch us. It would be so easy to kill us both right now, to spare himself this trouble of mating us. I lean closer to Danny, and he takes a step back, alarmed, then smiles and moves closer. Dave watches, dropping ashes onto the brochures spread across his lap. He smiles. Perhaps we will be married by Christmas. His patience could not last much beyond that.

—So, Danny says, then nothing; we stand for a moment, then suddenly he turns and heads back to the couch. Dave watches, sighs, shakes his head. He looks down at the brochure on his lap; it is covered with ashes; he brushes them to the floor, and stares down at them. He must wonder why he is bothering with something that will matter so little to him in the long run.

I know I should be more cooperative; he is only trying to do for me what I will not do for myself, which is to improve upon my miserable prospects, and I should be grateful for that. My parents did not take such interest in the progress of our lives. My mother was more or less waiting for me to blossom, and every now and then, when she noticed that I was failing to do so, she sent me to something or other, some place she had seen people my age gathering–to some carnival, or mall, or wherever she had seen children gather. She always dropped me by the side of the road, and I stood there until her car was out of sight, and then I sat down and waited for her to pick me up several hours later. I spent the time thinking of my sister, imagining her at home alone sitting at her little table, looking at herself, thinking of the boys I was talking to, the friends I was making–all the things I was gathering for myself that should have belonged to her. I never talked to anyone, but still it felt as if I were betraying her, just by being there. When I got home, my sister would not look at me; sometimes she would not even come out of the bathroom.

My mother's efforts were halfhearted and sporadic, and after a while ceased entirely, so that I was more or less left alone throughout high school; her interest revived only enough to send me to college and write out her list of places for me to visit. My father's single interest was television, but even that seemed hardly a real interest, but rather something to occupy his eyes while they were open. I used to wonder sometimes what he did at his job: if he arrived, hung up his jacket, then sat at his desk and laid his hands on his knees, and stared numbly at some fixed point while business went on around him. I don't know what he looked at when he was in bed with my mother; perhaps a distant speck of light in her eye, or the moon in the sky beyond her head. Or perhaps it was something more prosaic: a slipper, a wadded-up tissue unnoticed on the floor, the streak of light from the hallway. He must have hated all of us in some way, but by the time I left, he was like something a guest had left behind in a chair, waiting for its retrieval—insensible and without any expectation or experience beyond the dull inert moment. He sat in his chair waiting for whatever it was he thought might one day occur. We were all waiting for something, and in the meantime our lives went on as though it did not matter that we were waiting for something. I never knew what it was. When my sister died, I thought that might have been what we were waiting for, but nothing at all changed.

My parents knew nothing of my sister and the boys who followed her; they knew nothing of what went on in our room, what it was like between us, how we spent our evenings. Sometimes, when I left our room to get a drink of water or to go to the bathroom, I returned to find the door immovable, barricaded by the dresser she'd shoved up against it, and on the other side I could hear her, perched on top of the dresser, her quick breaths beating against the air like moths against glass. I would go downstairs to the living room then to watch television with my parents, and after a while I would return to my room to find it as I had left it, the dresser back in its normal position and my sister lying on her bed, her face half-covered with a pillow or blanket as she read a magazine, pretending not to hear me enter, or to see me cross in front of her to get to my bed, only a few feet away.

After the last customer has left, Danny comes to the counter. He holds his popcorn bag out; he has folded it into a damp oily triangle and I look down at it. He follows my eyes.

—Oh, he says. —Sorry. He drops the bag on the counter as Dave comes down the stairs from the projection room.

—Okay, Dave says heartily, to no one, then stops in the middle of the lobby and stares at us both.

—Well, I say to Danny as I come around the counter and head for the door. —It was nice to meet you.

—Hey, Dave says, —he can walk you.

He gives Danny a little shove in my direction and Danny stumbles toward me, then follows me out, somehow entangling himself in the glass door before Dave wrests it from his grasp and closes it. He watches us from behind the door as we walk away; he is watching us still as we turn the corner, his face pressed against the glass, peering out like an abandoned child.

At the Hygienic, Danny's eyes move from the junkies to the hookers to the drag queens, then back again, around and around the room. A hooker is standing in the corner wearing white hot pants and a red halter top, despite the chill, and she is long past her prime. Even from here, I can see the purple veiny blotches in her face and legs, and the knotty tendons at her joints. Danny's eyes keep coming back to rest on her before they circle the room again. I watch him in the mirror. Our faces are reflected together in a clear stretch of glass, unwarped, and from the look of us, we could be any normal young couple stopping off for a bite after an evening's entertainment. From here, we would drive home to our sleeping children, our pets. We would send our baby-sitter home, then watch television until we climbed the stairs to bed. Danny would turn and fumble for me with his big hands. When I closed my eyes to kiss him, the feathers of a thousand pigeons would fall on us, drifting over our pillows, our sheets, scattering over our bodies like rain. Outside, my sister would press her ear against our door.

Danny's hands rest innocently on the table now, in front of him, one on top of the other; he looks up as the waitress sloshes coffee into our cups, then drops menus on the table in front of us. Danny reads his menu carefully, his eyes slowly traveling down one side, then the other. He lays it on the table with a sat-isfied sigh just as Jerome enters, and he watches Jerome until it becomes clear that we are his destination. He looks quickly at me, alarmed, but Jerome is suddenly teetering above us. He is looking a little ragged—his makeup blotchy, his dress wrin-kled—and he stares down at us.

—Well, he says. —Even you have a date tonight. He shakes his head. —Scoot over, honey, he says and slides in next to me. He sighs, then reaches over me for a packet of Sweet 'n Low, which he tears open and pours out onto the table; he gazes at the little white heap, then dips his finger into it and delicately touches his finger to the tip of his tongue. His nail polish is chipped at the edges, and under the scent of perfume is a musky male smell.

Danny has opened his menu again, and stares fixedly down at it, moving his hand up and down over the selections as he reads. Jerome watches him for a while; then, as the waitress passes, he waves his hand grandly at her.

—Oh, Miss, he says autocratically, and she stops, her pencil to her pad, her eyes on the floor. —Coffee, please, Jerome says, as if he is ordering the most expensive wine in the house. —And the cottage cheese.

Danny keeps his head down, but glances up at him, and when Jerome turns back to the table, Danny's eyes dart back to the menu.

—Well, Jerome says, looking at Danny as if he has just this moment materialized. —Who have you been hiding here?

When I introduce them, Danny just looks up and nods nervously, but Jerome gives him a dazzling movie-star smile, and holds his hand out across the table. —Charmed, he says. His hand hovers by Danny's mouth, and Danny stares at it, bewildered. After a moment, Jerome leans forward and touches his fingers to Danny's lips; Danny jerks back, his face flushing, but Jerome only bats his eyes.

—He's a shy one, he says to me, his eyes still on Danny. He winks. —I just love a shy man, he says. He leans back and gazes at Danny as the waitress puts coffee in front of him.

—Danny, Jerome breathes, as if he is saying "Heaven." He leans forward again. I can tell the tree question is coming.

When it does, Danny stares at Jerome openmouthed, then looks at me. I shrug.

—I said "birch," I say.

—Birch, Danny says.

Jerome smiles and sits back with a rapturous sigh. —Birch, he repeats, gazing at Danny; then he shakes his head. —No, he says, —not birch. He looks at me.

—What are them big things? he asks. —With all the leaves?

—Oak? I say, and he looks back at Danny.

—Oak, Jerome says. —That's what you are, he says. —A big strong oak tree. He sighs. —I bet you're strong, he says. —Look at those big strong hands—and we all look down at Danny's hands. His fingers are splayed out gently over his menu. They twitch a bit under our scrutiny, and Jerome reaches out toward him, but Danny pulls his hands away, into his lap.

—I don't bite, honey, Jerome says.

His smile fades when Eric enters. He is alone tonight, and stands in the doorway, looking around the room. His eyes fall on us briefly, then keep moving, and after a moment he walks straight over to the hooker. Jerome watches him. Eric says something to the woman, then reaches his hand out and runs his finger across her breast, right over the nipple. For a moment, I think I see her flinch; then she drops her cigarette, steps on it, and smiles at him. Jerome stands.

—Excuse me, honey, he says to Danny. —I've got business to take care of. He sweeps off toward Eric, and Danny looks at me.

—He's really very nice, I say, and Danny turns to watch Jerome. At first he stands a few feet away from Eric and the hooker, watching, but when Eric ignores him, turning his back and whispering something in the woman's ear, Jerome steps forward and puts his hand on Eric's arm. Eric turns and looks at him; his face is as placid as a dog's, but suddenly he swats out, his hand flashing against Jerome's face. I can hear the smack, and I look away from them, into the mirror at their reflections. They stare at each other while the hooker looks on, uninvolved. After a moment Eric takes her by the arm, and they leave. Jerome watches them go, then heads for the counter and maneuvers into a stool next to a junkie. The junkie glares at him, and slips from his stool and onto the next one, his arm held protectively around his food, sliding it down the counter with him. I look back at Danny. He is staring at me.

—He's really very nice, I say, and he gazes down at his hands in front of him on the table.

—He's an orphan, I say, and Danny looks up, then turns to watch Jerome pull a compact and a tube of lipstick from his purse.

—An orphan? he repeats, staring as Jerome opens the compact and applies lipstick.

—He lives in a home, I say, and Danny looks back at me.

—A home? he breathes. He looks back around at Jerome, who blots his lips on a napkin, then moves to a seat next to a sailor at the counter.

The waitress brings Jerome's cottage cheese, glances at him across the room, but sets it down on the table anyways, where it sits between us like an unsaid thought.

When we leave, Jerome is sitting in the sailor's lap; the sailor's white cap is perched jauntily on top of Jerome's bright-red wig. —Well, Danny says as we stand outside looking in. Jerome sees us watching and blows Danny a kiss. Danny looks at the ground, then at me. —Well, he says again. —I really enjoyed meeting you. I really did.

He holds his hand out, and I shake it. His palm is warm and pillowy, and he looks down at our hands a moment, then drops mine and says, —Well, one more time before he turns and leaves.

I glance back inside; someone has already taken our booth, though Jerome's cottage cheese still sits in a perfect round scoop in the middle of the table.

Danny disappears around the corner. When he arrives at the theater, he will glance in and see Dave at the popcorn machine; he will tap at the glass, and Dave will look up, still chewing, then let him in.

No one will ever love you, my sister says. *No one could ever love you. Only I could love you. You will always be alone.*

I close my eyes. Across the dark sea between us, she leans to me. *Everyone will love me,* she whispers. *I am the one they will love.*

I sink and surface and sink again to the sound of her voice and the brush of her hand over my face, crossing the skin, the eyes, moving over the rise and fall of bone. I shudder and jerk from sleep to find my hand on my mouth.

—Debbie, the man next door is saying. —Debbie. His voice is urgent and mournful both. —Debbie, he says again. At the theater, Danny and Dave have reached the bottom of the popcorn machine; they gaze blankly down at the metal plate. There is nothing left.

Danny is waiting for me when I come in the next day. I see him from a block away, hovering behind the doors of the theater. He steps back as I enter. The popcorn is already in the machine, my bubble already lit, the lights already on; everything I do has been done. There is nothing but to take my place in my bubble as Danny ambles across the lobby to the couch.

Dave hurries from his office to the stairs before the first customer has even come, giving me a quick wave, and I lean back with a magazine. Danny watches me alertly, like a dog waiting to be taken for a walk. His shoulders move as he breathes; I can hear his breath across the room.

—So, Dave says, after the show has begun. I look up from the magazine article I am reading; it is about a woman who spent a year by herself in a cave—it was an underground room, really, with walls and lights and an electric generator. She was a psychologist conducting an experiment; the room had been built just for this. She killed herself a year after she came out of the cave, on the exact date of the anniversary of her release.

—So, Dave says again. —Nice kid, huh? We both look over at Danny. When he sees us looking at him, he looks quickly around behind him, then flushes when he realizes it is him we are watching.

I nod. —Yes, I say. —And quite a speller.

Dave gazes at me a moment, gauging, then nods. —Well, he says. —Good.

He heads back to his office, nodding all the way, then leaves the door open as he takes his seat, leaning back to look out at us. All evening he watches us to see what happens, but what happens is nothing at all. Every now and then, Danny approaches me for popcorn, then returns to his couch, chewing. We do not have any conversations. Dave shakes his head.

Between visits from Danny and stray customers at my window, I finish the article about the woman in the cave. She kept a diary, both during her time in the cave and after. It was only when she emerged, she wrote, that she saw how disjointed her thoughts had become in the cave; toward the end, she had found herself thinking of things that had never interested her before–things like automobile engines, ladders, football. She spent almost an entire week thinking of elephants, nothing but elephants; she said she spent hours on the ears alone. She had taken a number of things with her to occupy her time, and at first she was busy, reading books, doing little tasks, keeping track of the experiment, but after a while she found that all she could do was think. At some point she even stopped keeping track of time, so that when they finally opened up her cave and let her out, she was not expecting it. She tried to record her dreams as well, but after a month or two, she said all she ever dreamed of was air, and what it would be like to breathe it. She forgot what sunlight was, she said, though she thought about it every day; it was the one thing she wanted to see again, but when she finally emerged, she found she could not bear it.

Danny watches everything I do, and when I leave, he stays behind with Dave; the two of them stand side by side in the doorway, watching me walk away, like two cardboard cutouts propped up against the glass.

Jerome comes early to the Hygienic tonight; he is wearing the same outfit he wore last night. A large yellowish stain spreads all the way across the front of his dress, and his hair is in a wild cloud around his head.

—Girl, he says, sitting across from me in the booth. —Have I had a time of it. He shakes his head, then slumps back, gazing blankly around the room, but when the waitress comes, he sits up straight, and gives me a crazy look.

—A hot fudge sundae, he blurts. —Bring me a hot fudge sundae. He smiles wildly at me, but before the waitress has even walked away, he stops her and changes his order to cottage cheese. As he turns his head at the sound of the door opening, I can see a long thin strip of stubble he has missed with the razor, running from his cheek all the way down his neck. When the waitress brings his cottage cheese, he stares down at it a moment, then sighs and picks up his fork and begins to eat.

In the mirror, there is a shape that looks like Danny, a shadow looming in the glass, but when I turn to look, there is nothing there. Jerome eats, swallows, eats, swallows, all without chewing; the line of stubble on his neck gleams with the movement of his muscles.

It is morning and a murky rain is falling. *The weather is nice here,* I write my parents, *sunny and cool.* To one side of me is the staticky hiss of the radio.

—No, listen, someone is saying as he is repeatedly interrupted by the host. —No, listen, he repeats. —Listen.

Every now and then, I hear the voice of my neighbor rising to curse at whatever people are saying on the radio, and on my other side I hear —Debbie, Debbie, Debbie. On a ledge outside my window, pigeons huddle together for dry warmth. They are safe for now from Danny's pigeon project, though tomorrow or the day after may find them beating their wings at a wall of wire mesh, pressing their breasts against it to escape, or to try to return inside.

I have met someone, I write. *He is studying to be a veterinarian.* I erase *veterinarian* and replace it with *doctor. Perhaps a plastic surgeon,* I add. *Doctor,* my mother will read, and smile for a moment before she looks up at my father, sitting innocently in his chair, not thinking, for just this moment, of the disappointment he has caused her with his career as a middle manager, which has given her so little in exchange for all she gave up. After a moment, he will sense her eyes on him; he will bury himself deeper into his chair, sink his hands deeper into his knees. *He is from a good family,* I write, which is something that will matter to my mother. It was the only thing she ever asked me about the one or two friends I acquired. I always told her yes, though I knew nothing about their families. It hardly seemed to matter what I told her, since my friendships lasted only briefly. Whenever my sister saw me with anyone, she would put herself a few yards away from us, and sit staring at us with an unnerving steadiness that usually drove the other girl away. And then, when I was left sitting alone, my sister would stay where she was, but turn away from me, humming to herself as though I were not there.

He is from a good family, I write, and then I realize I have already written this. I cross it out.

He drives a yellow sports car, I add to the letter. The car is something my sister would have envied, and I suppose it is for her sake that I add it. She would have lain awake over it, on fire with wanting it for herself, until she would have reminded herself that it could not be true, that no man could love me. No one could love me.

Danny is the first man I have written them about, though I have told them of other friends, particularly my roommate. *We are inseparable,* I wrote them when I first came to the college, *like sisters.*

I will be spending Christmas with her again this year, I add to my letter now. This is what I told them last year. *Her family welcomed me like their own child,* I wrote in my letter. *There were presents for everyone, and sleigh rides, and a stable full of horses.* My sister was alive then, and for her I wrote about the horse who was mine for the holiday, a large white one named Tony. *I groomed and fed him every day,* I said, and I described the way I could hold a piece of apple between my teeth, and he would take it directly from my own mouth with his. *He was as gentle as a rabbit,* I told her, *and his breath was like a warm fog against my face. His lips were as soft as a feather.* Whenever I see a picture of a horse in one of Dave's magazines, I think about Tony, how smooth his coat was, the way it felt to run my hand down the solid ridge of his neck, and then I remember that I have never touched a horse. *It was the most wonderful holiday imaginable,* I wrote.

In fact, I spent the holiday at the school, with the few other girls who did not go home. There was a girl from Mexico, a skinny girl from some Southern state, and two others, roommates, who never spoke to me, so I knew nothing about them. Our building was kept open, and meals were provided, but we had no supervision and were left to do what we chose. The two roommates were together always, and the other two, like me, seemed to spend most of their time in their rooms alone. I saw them all only at meals we shared at a table that was set for us in the dining room. Women served us, then hovered at the glass window of the door to the kitchen, watching us eat. They were the only staff I saw the whole time. The bathroom was cleaned every day, but I never saw anyone do it, as though it was cleaned by ghosts. At every meal, the girls prayed, both before and after they ate, while I bowed my head and watched them from the corner of my eye. Even the girl from Mexico seemed transformed by the prayer, her usually sullen face suffused with a glowing fervor. We didn't talk much at meals; the girl from the South ate quickly and constantly, hardly swallowing between bites, then wrapping any leftover food up in paper napkins, even half-eaten messy things, and stuffing it all in her pockets; the two roommates exchanged secret little looks and occasional whispers. The girl from Mexico spoke almost no English, and seldom attempted it. I couldn't imagine how she had gotten there, who had sent her, or why.

On Christmas Eve, someone thought to provide us with Christmas presents, which sat in identically shaped and wrapped little boxes at our places. We all looked at them, but no one moved to open hers, until finally the girl from Mexico picked hers up and shook it, then ripped off the wrapping. Inside the box was a little cheap aluminum cross, with a tiny aluminum Jesus stuck to it, hanging from an aluminum chain. The girl stared at the cross a moment, then closed the box back up and put it by her plate. The cross she already wore around her neck was much more elaborate and expensive—made of real gold, and hanging from a heavy gold chain. The Jesus on her cross was silver, with little rubies holding his hands and feet down; a trail of tears made of tiny diamonds ran down the side of his face.

One by one, the other girls opened their boxes, looked at their identical crosses, and laid them aside. I left mine unopened by my plate as I ate, and though they knew it was the same as theirs, the other girls glanced jealously at it from time to time, even during the after-dinner prayer. I opened it in my room later, and although I knew what it was going to be, I still felt a faint sigh of disappointment when I saw it. I thought of sending it to my sister, but instead put it around my neck. The little Jesus came off after a few days. I never found it, and now the cross hangs from the doorknob of my room. It makes a tinny rattle when I open the door.

—Fuck, the man next door says, —fucking Jesus Christ. He snaps off the radio, but after a moment he turns it back on.

I get up to go to the bathroom, but Debbie's owner is at the sink, rinsing and refilling Debbie's water dish. He has left his own door open, and just inside, Debbie hunches by the wall, her ears flat out at the sides, her eyes closed. She could be sleeping except for the quick shallow breaths that come from her slightly open mouth. Her fur lies in greasy strips along her back. I crouch down.

—Debbie, I say, and her ears flick, but her eyes stay closed. Her owner looks sharply around at me and turns the water off quickly.

—Excuse me, he says loudly, and comes down the hall toward me, dripping water on the floor behind him. —*Excuse* me, he says again, and I stand.

—I was just looking at your cat, I say. —She seems a little sick. We both stare at Debbie a moment, all hunched into herself; she is oblivious to our attention. Her owner looks down at the bowl he is always filling.

—She's fine, he snaps suddenly, then edges around in front of me, holding the bowl out at his chest, like a weapon to keep me at bay. His face is thin and worried, and he looks as if he exists on nothing but water himself; his skin is as pale as water. As he backs into his room, he keeps his eyes on me, and pulls the door to; he pauses before it closes.

—And besides, he says. —It's none of your business. You should have better things to do than bother people's pets.

I go into my room, lie down, and lean my head against the wall, listening to the lap-lap of water as Debbie drinks. I close my eyes. I will have a cat of my own one day who will sit on my lap every evening. I will name her Annabelle, and she will be all mine, and at night she will sleep on the pillow next to my head, her furry soft paws pressed against my cheek.

—Jesus *fucking* Christ, the man next door says, and I jerk suddenly against the wall, with the sourness of a moment's half-sleep in my mouth and the quick thump of my heart. I am stiff when I stand, though I have dozed here only a moment. Outside, the rain has let up a little, giving way to a spitty sleet. In the alley below my window, the manager's wife is crouching by the Dumpster, staring out into the street. She spends most of her days there, and if it weren't for what she was doing, she might pass as any normal person out for a stroll: she looks and dresses normally; she always carries a purse and sometimes even wears matching pumps. Every now and then, she scuttles to the mouth of the alley and jumps out suddenly into the path of some passerby, but for the most part, she seems to just sit and wait.

I was surprised the first time I saw her inside the building, lurking by the stairs, and even more surprised when I asked the manager to replace a broken bulb and he jerked his head at her and said, —That's her job—the wife's, then went back to his paper. He said "wife" as if he were saying "rat," or "cockroach." The bulb went unreplaced. It's hard to imagine them co-existing, getting through the daily things like waking up in the same room, brushing their teeth, sharing meals, two people who seem so full of hate and craziness.

Once or twice, she has called out at me. —Hey, you, she says. —Hey, but I always keep going.

A shadow looms at the glass doors of the theater; from a few blocks away, it looks like an image seared into the glass, but it is only Danny, who opens the door for me, blushing as he steps back to let me enter.

Dave comes out of his office and gives me a little wave; then they both watch me walk to my bubble as if I were a child taking its first steps. Everything is ready for me and I go into my bubble. Danny takes his seat on the couch and when I look at him, he smiles pleasantly. He is not so bad, I tell myself, not so bad at all. He is a nice boy. I think of saying this out loud to someone. He is a nice boy. My sister would stare at me a moment, then snort. Nice boy, she would say, he probably lives with his mother, and she would probably be right—he is the kind of boy who would live with his mother and she would be the kind of mother who would dote on him, who irons his shirts and hovers over him while he eats, wondering when he is going to leave her and for whom. And when she sends him off to his job, she does not think about what it is he does all day, sealing off feathery bundles of pigeons into their tunnels of gas. He is her son, and he loves her. He could not hurt a fly.

I turn from Danny and handle the small rush of tickets for the first show, then lean back in my chair. I close my eyes and try to see Danny in a yellow sports car. It's a stretch. I give him new clothes, new hair, a new shape; I change nearly everything and put him behind the wheel; he opens the door for me, but before I can get to him, my sister is there. She is wearing sunglasses and a long blue scarf. She is glamorous. Her face is beautiful. She gives Danny a dazzling smile, and as they drive off she waves back at me. *No one will ever love you,* she calls out. *You will always be alone.* Her blue scarf trails behind them in the bright blue air.

I look at Danny. The floor around him is covered with popcorn. He has popcorn on his shirt and legs, and somehow bits of it have got stuck in his hair.

—Hey, someone says behind me, and I turn. It's Eric. His face is a few inches from the glass, and he gives me an oily smile, but seems not to recognize me. A woman stands behind him; she is heavily made up, her face a mask of boredom. Eric makes a grab for my fingers as I pass the tickets and take his money, but I pull the money away too fast, and he laughs and winks; the woman follows him in with no apparent interest in our exchange, and I sit back with a magazine, but in a moment a loud rapping comes from behind me and I turn; Eric is knocking the back of his hand against the glass candy counter, his rings rattling the glass sharply.

—Hey, he says. —Gimme some of that popcorn. And she—he
tosses his head in the direction of the woman, who is standing
a few feet from Danny, examining one of the posters—wants
some candy. He peers down through the glass at the candy
selection.

—Dots, he says. He leans forward on the glass.

—So, he says. —Where you been all my life? I can feel his eyes
on my body as I turn for the popcorn. I can feel all of their eyes:
his, Danny's, Dave's. As I scoop popcorn into the bag, I feel like
an insect crawling up a wall, waiting for the slap of a hand.

I put the bag of popcorn in front of him and bend for the Dots;
he watches, then leans his head over the bag and picks up a
piece of popcorn with the tip of his tongue. His tongue is
bluish, with yellow dots all around the edge. He smiles and
swallows the popcorn whole, then winks and drops a few dollar
bills on the counter before he turns to retrieve the woman. As
they walk into the theater, he tosses a piece of popcorn into the
air, but makes only a halfhearted attempt to catch it in his
mouth, and the popcorn bounces on the floor behind them.
Danny stares at it a long moment, shifts uneasily, then stands
and walks rather aimlessly across the lobby, looking around as
if he is just taking a stroll, admiring the decor; he stops at the
popcorn, and casually bends to pick it up; there is no garbage
can near him, only an ashtray already crammed full of butts.
He glances quickly at me, but I keep my head down, watching
him over my magazine, and finally he stuffs the popcorn into
his pocket. *He is very neat,* I remind myself to tell my mother.
Danny goes back to his couch, and I flip through the magazine
to the story about the woman in the cave. There are two photographs of her, one taken just before her descent into the cave,
one just as she emerged. Her husband is in both pictures; in the
first, he is gazing at her proudly, but she has already turned to
begin her descent and only the side of her face is visible. Coming out, her face is as flat as a plate, pale from lack of light, and

though she is looking directly into the camera, her eyes seem to have disappeared; they are like little black stones. Her husband stands next to her, watching anxiously; he reaches for her, and though she seems not even to have seen him, it looks as if she is shrinking away from his grasp. I tear out the page with the pictures, then carefully rip the husband away and tape up the two pictures of the woman, side by side.

She has been dead several months now. She might as well have died underground, is what she wrote in the diary she kept after she came out of the cave. When she first came out of the cave, she wrote, she thought that she was safe, but then after only a few weeks, all she thought about was dying: how she would die, when she would die, what time of day it would be, if the sun would shine the day of her funeral. It was easier just to do it herself, she said, instead of worrying about it all the time.

The sun did not shine the day of my sister's funeral. It was neither cloudy nor bright; a gloomy hazy sun shone down on us. We were not the only funeral that day, but we were the smallest, and I remember standing by the grave and wondering why my parents had gone to such trouble for something only the three of us attended. On the drive home, my mother gazed out the window, smoking, and my father stared intently straight ahead. I sat in the back seat. It seemed as if nothing at all had happened. My sister's room had been cleaned and emptied before my arrival, her pictures taken from the wall, her clothes packed into a small box, which my mother gave to me. We were the same size, she said; I might as well have them. I put it into the trunk of my car and left that night; I had an early class, I told my mother, and I had to get back and study. I kept the box in the trunk of my car until I moved into my room, and now it is here, in the tiny closet.

My sister would have hated for me to have her things; I was too ugly to be her sister, she always said, though we looked so much alike. One day, she used to tell me, she would find her real sister, who was beautiful. This used to drive me to the mirror, but all I could ever see was skin—skin and an assortment of the usual features, but not exactly anything that made a face. I could not have described what I looked like to someone who had never seen me.

One day I came home from school and our mirror was gone, in its place just a faintly lighter square of paint on the wall. And in the bathroom, the mirror on the medicine cabinet had been neatly taped over with black electrical tape. My sister lay on her bed reading a fashion magazine, not acknowledging my presence except to turn on her side away from me. She said nothing about the mirror, but several days later I found it under my bed, broken into several large sharp pieces; it made me uneasy to think that I had slept over it for a few nights, and I picked up the largest pieces and put them in the garbage.

Nothing was ever said about the mirror, and later the rest of the smaller pieces were gone too, vacuumed up by my mother, I suppose, when she cleaned our room. We lived like vampires after that, without reflections, and after a time of dressing and brushing my teeth and washing my face without seeing my face, it became unnerving to catch sight of myself in a mirror at school, or in a window; it was like getting a glimpse of another world, a world that everyone who looked at me could see but that I could not.

Though the mirror was gone years before my sister died, I always thought of it as having something to do with her death; for a long time I dreamed of her falling on it, the sharp edges of it driving into her heart.

—It was an accident, was all my mother said when my sister died, —a terrible accident. Then she shook her head and lit a cigarette and looked off a moment before she turned again to gaze at my father in disappointment.

Sometimes I think of my sister's face, reflected a thousand times, scattered across the floor under my bed, her sharp little eyes, her teeth. There are nights when I wake with my hand on my face, and I am not sure for a long time whose hand it is, even when I have fully awakened.

Danny yawns loudly, and I look up at him. He smiles, stretches his arms up over his head, then puts his hands back on his lap. His face is pleasant and tranquil; I think of his hands on my face, his lips against mine.

His mouth would be soft and pillowy, like his hand. When my sister died, I thought: Now I will not have to save her, and when I thought that, I felt a spider run across my heart, and then another. Spiders run across my heart still, and if I close my eyes, I can hear the rush and rustle of their tiny dry bodies scurrying through me. Up on the hill, the girls turn to the sky and pray. They are praying for the souls of people like me, people whose hearts are consumed by spiders. They pray for all of us, their soft round faces turned all in a row to God, like flowers turning to the light, and God rouses himself for a moment to hear them. He listens only to the voices of people who have already given themselves to him, the voices of the saved. He listens, then slumbers back asleep. He does not have to help those who are already saved. The rest of us do not deserve his attention.

My roommate prayed with extra fervor for those who were not saved, especially those who would never be saved; if she ever heard about anyone anywhere about to be executed, she prayed for him loudly, and even more loudly when he was dead. I tried praying for my sister after she died. I followed the lead of my roommate: down on my knees, face turned to the sky, but when I closed my eyes, I could not speak. Spiders crept from my heart to fill my mouth; I imagined how my sister would laugh to see me there on my knees, and when I opened my eyes, there was nothing there, only stars, the sky, the moon.

Danny smiles pleasantly as he rearranges himself on the couch. When I take him to meet my parents, he will smile pleasantly at my mother, gazing at her from where he sits at his tray in front of the television; she will sense his eyes on her and turn to him. Our honeymoon will last forever. Outside, a little band of drag queens heads up the street; Jerome is not with them.

When Eric leaves, he veers over toward me; he winks and makes a little clicking sound out of the side of his mouth. Danny watches alertly until he is out of sight, then sits back, his hands on his knees.

After he starts the last show, Dave comes to join me and leans on the counter with me, watching Danny. When Danny becomes aware of our gaze, he glances around, moves his feet, puts one arm across the back of the couch, then the other, then brings them both back to his lap, and finally collapses into himself, in a kind of slumping heap.

—I told you, Dave says. —I told you he was a little goofy.

—I know, I say. —Goofy in a nice way.

—Well, he says, —maybe you've got something better lined up? I can tell he regrets the words the minute they're out. He stares at the floor a moment, then pulls out his cigarettes and offers me one, though he knows I don't smoke. He sighs, and starts off toward his office, then turns.

—I know, he says. —Dinner. He nods, then barks it out at Danny: —*Dinner.*

Danny looks up, startled, and Dave repeats it slowly, as if he is teaching him a new word: —Din-ner.

Dave looks at me. —You like steak, don't you? he asks, then answers himself, —Sure you do. Everybody likes steak. And pie. Apple pie.

—Cherry, I say, and he looks at me a long moment.

—Sure, he says finally. —What the hell. Cherry. He turns back
to his office.
—Sunday, he says over his shoulder.
Danny watches Dave go into his office, and then he turns his
gaze back to me. He watches like a dog—watching without actually watching, but if I were to move, he would know it.

Jerome is already at the Hygienic when I arrive; he is nearly
seven feet tall in the heels he's wearing, and decked out in some
sort of huge pink fuzzy cape-like thing and his bright-red wig.
He stands in the corner, surrounded by three or four sailors,
and waves dramatically to me across the room. I wave back and
sit at a booth.
Eric is at the counter; he is still with the woman he brought to
the theater, but he has turned on his stool to watch Jerome. He
watches him awhile, then scans the room; his eyes stop at me.
Quickly I take from my coat the letter I have begun to my parents and bend over it, pretending to be absorbed in writing, but
he is at my table in a moment, and slides in across from me.
—Well, hey there, beautiful, he says. —Remember me? I look
up and shake my head.
—Sure you do, he says.
He leans across the table, then reaches his hand out, brushing
his fingers against my cheek before I can jerk my head away.
—Ha, he says. —Hard to get.
He puts his hands on the table in front of him, and taps on the
top as if he is drumming. His fingers are long and stained yel-
low at the tips. I bend to my letter.
—Whatcha writin? he asks.
—A letter, I say, and he cocks his head to try to read it. I cover
it with my hand.
—It's to my sister, I say, and he nods. —She's a stewardess, I
add, and he raises his eyebrows, impressed.

Across the room, Jerome is watching us closely; one of the sailors has his arm around Jerome's waist, and the others are grinning at one another, but Jerome breaks away and heads for our table. He looms brightly over us, swaying slightly on his thin heels.

—Baby, he says to Eric, —I wondered where you was. He reaches his hand out and runs his nails along Eric's neck. Eric swats his hand away and Jerome giggles. —Oh, you, he says.

Eric ignores him, and leans forward on his elbows, looking at me. Jerome sways above us a moment, then suddenly drops onto the seat next to Eric. Eric does not shift to give him room, and Jerome has to perch awkwardly sideways; he turns his long neck to gaze at Eric, who has not taken his eyes from me.

—I missed you, baby, Jerome says.

—She was just writing a *letter*, Eric says. —To her sister.

—Humph, Jerome says. —I'd never write my sister. He pauses.

—That bitch, he adds. He huffs a bit, and smoothes his dress out over his knees. As he moves, the fuzzy edge of the cape catches Eric in the ear, and Eric bats at it, then moves away from Jerome, who scoots back even closer to him.

This is the first I have heard of a sister. —Where is she? I ask, and Jerome looks at me a long time, then waves his hand dismissively.

—She's a receptionist, he says. —For a dentist. That bitch.

This seems too ordinary not to be true, that Jerome has a sister somewhere who is a receptionist for a dentist. Perhaps she lives with Jerome's parents; perhaps they have pleasant happy lives, pretending that Jerome does not exist. Perhaps they tell themselves that he died in a plane crash or a dramatic car accident, and that his body was never recovered.

Eric jerks his head at me. —*Her* sister's a stewardess, he says, as if he trained her himself.

Jerome looks jealously at my letter. —Well, he says finally, —I could have been a stewardess. I was just too tall. He touches his hand delicately to the back of his hair and looks around the room.

Eric grins at me. —I bet you're not too tall, he says, and Jerome turns to look sharply at him.

—Well, I say, standing, —I'd better get this mailed.

They both look up at me, but before I can move, Eric's date from the movie has come to the booth and stands next to me, looking down at Eric.

—Well, she says. —Are we done?

Jerome stares up at her a moment, then stands, towering over her.

—Excuse me, honey, he says. He pushes past her and sashays across the room and out the door. Eric stares straight ahead, not turning to watch him leave, but the sailors in the corner are watching Jerome, and after a moment, they follow him out. The last one in the group gives the man in front of him a little shove, so that he bumps into the man in front of him, and they all stumble out, laughing.

—Well, I say again, —off to the post office, though it is something like 2 a.m. Neither Eric nor the woman respond, and I leave; at the door, I realize I've left my letter. When I look back, the woman is gone, and Eric is still at the table, staring straight ahead. My letter sits on the table in front of him. I leave it there. Jerome is just across the street, and he is surrounded by the group of sailors; in the dark, their heads and faces glow like little white moons. They have formed a circle around him, slowly moving, laughing, while Jerome looks coyly from one to the next.

—Jerome, I call, and the sailors turn to look at me, losing interest in Jerome for a moment.

—Hey, sweetheart, one of them calls. —Come on over here. He has a soft, sweet Southern voice, but his face is mean-looking.

—Jerome, I say again.

—Jeroooome, one of the sailors mocks. They have all turned to look at me now.

Jerome stares at me coldly. —Go on, he says. —I don't know you. You get out of here.

He taps the nearest sailor on the shoulder, and the sailor turns back to him. Jerome bats his eyes, and the rest of the sailors turn too, closing back in.

I go straight to my building. Anything at all could happen now.

Even after I have washed my face and brushed my teeth and turned out my light, I can still feel the touch of Eric's fingers on my cheek. Beautiful, he said.

Beautiful, my sister says from the shadows: *you are beautiful. Come to me.*

On Sunday, Danny picks me up at the address I have given him, an apartment building several blocks from my hotel.

—Nice place, he says when I get in the car, and I nod. I tell him my neighbors are interior decorators. They have a beautiful apartment, I say, full of paintings and antiques. Each room is painted a different color.

—And they have a cat, I add. —Debbie.

He nods. —Debbie, he says. —Debbie's a nice name.

We drive for a while in silence. He is dressed up, wearing a green-and-red striped tie; he flushes when he sees me looking at it.

—Nice tie, I say.

He looks down at it. —I don't wear ties much, he says. —Mostly uniforms. —Green, he adds, and I nod. —Shirts and pants, he says. —The same color green. We are leaving the city limits now, passing through a section full of lots and empty warehouses.

—Well, I say after a moment, —green is a nice color.

—I know, he says. —I like green. But not as much as blue, he adds quickly, and I say that yes, blue is nice too.

If Danny and I were to marry, we might have fifty or sixty years of such talk. That brown chair is nice, he might one day say;

Yes, I would agree, brown is a good color for a chair. But the orange one is nice too, he would quickly add, and I would agree with that too. It could take us years to name a child. Well, one of us might suggest, Mary is a pretty name, and the other would nod and then add, after a pause, that Jane was also a very nice name, and so on. We would raise into adolescence a child without a name, prowling from room to room unnoticed, as we politely decided what to call her. By the time we finally settled on a name, she would have left us, and we could not even call her home, because she would not recognize the name we had given her in her absence. She would turn up in a town like this, and eventually, with nothing but a name to remember her by, we would let her fade from our thoughts, leaving us to sit side by side in our chairs and wonder one day if perhaps we should have a child to bring some life to the quiet rooms of our lives.

We spend the rest of the drive in silence, until we turn in to a modest housing tract. I grew up in one of these houses, one just like it. It's not a new development, built maybe in the 1950s or '60s, and while there are still lingering traces of promise—rows of bushes on the corners, and even a small park—mostly there is decay: buckling sidewalks, long cracks running down the wide streets, peeling paint and faded siding. It is decay, but the kind of modest decay that trails after modest people who are only just unable to keep up with the modest things they have acquired for themselves. Every house speaks of an overdue mortgage.

As we drive through the wide streets, most of them named for trees though there are few trees here, Danny slows at each crossing, peering up at the sign, then whispering the street name to himself before moving on. Finally, he pulls over and stares at a house with a neatly trimmed lawn and a yard full of little statues.

—I think this is it, he says. —I think that was the number.

—Haven't you been here before? I ask, and he shakes his head.

—Not really, he says. He cuts the engine and we get out. Most
of the lawn ornaments are animals–a small deer, its long neck
bent to nibble gracefully at the grass; a row of skunks by the
driveway; a tiny house surrounded by several plastic squirrels.
In the backyard a depressed-looking dog is attached by a short
chain to a battered little doghouse. When we walk into the yard,
it lets out a feeble yelp, then quickly looks around and slides
down into the dirt that surrounds the doghouse.
—Look, Danny says from behind me, —animals.
I nod, thinking he is talking about the dog in the yard, but
when I turn, he is patting the plastic deer on the neck.
I ring the doorbell, and when Dave answers, he stands in the
doorway a moment looking at me as if he has never seen me before. He looks past me at Danny, who is on his knees, peering
into the tiny house surrounded by squirrels.
—Hey, he snaps, and Danny stands and ambles over.
—Nice dog, I say, and Dave sighs.
—Blackie, he says. —My wife's. He glances into the house behind him. —My first wife's, he adds.
He stands back from the door. —Well, come on, he says.
Behind him there is a sudden crash of dishes, and Dave closes
his eyes a moment, but does not turn. —Well, he finally says,
—my wife is certainly anxious to meet you.
We all stand a moment longer, Dave blocking the door, and then
he turns abruptly, muttering as he goes, —Oh well, come on in,
and we follow him into a small living room. Magazines are
stacked everywhere, mostly fashion magazines. The carpet is a
blend of colors that defy any single category; it could keep
Danny and me busy for years, trying to agree on what color it is.
The walls are decorated with the kinds of paintings that hang
over the beds in motel rooms: pleasant vague landscapes that
could be anywhere at all. Dave steers us to the couch and
hems us in there until we sit, side by side. It is the closest I

have ever been to Danny. I can feel his breath vibrate through the couch.

—She's getting the drinks, Dave says; at the sound of another clatter from the kitchen, he sighs and leaves the room, throwing Danny and me into the sudden intimacy of a couple who has come for dinner. I sit back on the couch and try for a conversational tone, as if we were two guests just meeting at a cocktail party, the first to arrive.

—Nice place, I say, and he nods, looking around. —I like the carpet, I offer, and he looks down at it carefully, as if it were a rare artifact he has been asked to appraise.

—Yes, he finally says. —It's nice.

—So, I ask, —would you call that carpet brown or green? And he looks at it again, stricken. —Or gray? I add.

He takes a deep breath, lets it out. —Green? he says.

Dave comes back, followed by his wife. She is tiny, with the kind of stringy thinness you would say comes from nerves, and there is something off about her face, something wrong in the tight pull of her skin across her cheeks, the strained arch of her eyebrows.

—Myra, Dave mumbles; her hand is dry and so thin and fragile I can feel each bone where it connects to the others. We all look at each other in a long empty silence that ends only when Myra announces that she will be going to get the cocktails. Dave watches her go, then turns back to us and heaves a sigh that he seems not to notice even as it leaves his whole body slack and slumped back in his chair. He gazes at Danny and me, his eyes fixed so intently on the space between us that I finally have to look sideways to make sure there is nothing there.

—Well, I say finally, and Danny and Dave both look at me gratefully. I smile and they wait expectantly.

—Those are nice paintings, is what I finally come up with, and Dave drops his jaw, flabbergasted, then throws an irritated glance around the room. He would have expected more from me. These are paintings that could not even be called art.

—They're from some motel, he says. —She liked them.

I look at the paintings, trying to imagine Myra, lying on her motel bed, looking at the paintings and wanting them for her own. Then it occurs to me that the paintings, like Blackie, might be legacies of the first wife.

—Your wife? I ask, and he nods.

—Myra? I say, and he fixes his eyes on me, his face unreadable.

—Yeah, he says.

—Well, Danny says suddenly; he seems uneasy. —They certainly are—and he stops, then gazes from one painting to the next and back again—nice. They certainly are nice.

Dave nods tensely. His face is as tight as a fist, and he stares straight ahead until Myra returns. She is carrying a tray full of odd-looking drinks, foamy reddish things with parasols; a tiny plastic monkey hangs by its tail from the lip of each glass, and things appear to be floating around inside. We all stare at them as she balances the tray on top of a stack of magazines on the table.

—They're Polynesian, she says. She gazes down at them a moment. —I got the recipe from a magazine.

She sits down, then lifts a glass from the tray and we all do the same; my glass is sticky and damp. When we all have our drinks, Myra raises her glass and looks around blankly.

—Well, she finally says. —Cheers. We thunk our glasses together, bumping umbrellas. Danny's plastic monkey tumbles from the edge of his glass onto the carpet, and he looks down, mortified, then glances around. No one appears to have noticed, and he looks down again, then leaves the monkey there. All our monkeys are different colors. Mine is yellow. I bring my glass to my lips, but there are so many things in it, it's hard to drink, and I watch Myra and Dave: Dave puts his drink back on the table untouched, but Myra carefully removes her umbrella and folds it up, then lays it gently on the table. She leaves the monkey, sipping delicately around it.

I do the same. The drink is almost unbearably strong and unbearably sweet at the same time.

—Mmm, I say, and rest my glass on my knee, but Danny drinks half of his at once.

—Wow, he says. —This is great.

Myra smiles. The muscles in one cheek bunch up but the corner of her mouth does not move. —I know, she says and leans forward.

—Just between you and me, she says confidentially to Danny, —I added a little extra. She sits back. —Drinks you get from magazines can be so bland. She takes another sip of her drink. —You know what I mean, she says.

—Oh, Danny says, looking down into his drink. He drains it suddenly and sets his glass on the table, then glances at Dave's drink before he leans back against the couch with a satisfied sigh. I will get the recipe, I tell myself. I will get the recipe from Myra and make this drink often. I will comb novelty shops, searching for different kinds of little animals to put in them, and when we have finished with our drinks, we will give the little animals to our children to play with. I will listen always for the sound of choking.

We have sunk into another silence, punctuated by an occasional sigh. Finally, I offer another remark about the paintings. Dave snorts and turns to stare out the window, but Myra leans forward in her chair.

—Well, thank you, she says. —It's nice to see that some people have an appreciation for art.

—I like them too, Danny says, and Myra turns to him.

—Really? she says, almost coy, and he nods, then waves his hand in the general direction of a wall.

—Especially that one, he says. Myra looks behind her, then back at Danny.

—Which one? she asks and Danny looks startled, then points uncertainly at a seascape on the opposite wall. —That one, he says. —The farm.

Even Dave turns to look at the painting, and we all stare at it for a while, searching for any evidence of farm-like detail; it may be that he has taken the blue sea for some sort of field, the whitecaps for rows of sheep or cows. We all turn back to each other.

—Well, Myra says, —that's the nice thing about art. She stands. —I'll just check on dinner, she says, and puts our glasses back on the tray. Danny watches the drinks as she carries them away. When she is gone, Dave turns again and looks at the painting, then glares at Danny.

—Farm? he demands furiously. —Where the hell do you see a farm in that picture? He looks at me. —Do you see a farm? Do you see anywhere, on any of these walls, anything that looks like a farm?

I look around.

—I don't know, I say. —It's art. It can be anything.

Dave stares at me, apoplectic, but Danny turns to me with a look of tender gratitude, and resettles on the couch, a few inches closer to me. We will have paintings on all our walls: farms and rivers and mountains. The walls of our children's rooms will be painted with cows, and puppies, and ducks in little rows. There will be no paintings of people.

—Farm, Dave mutters, turning again to stare at each painting. Myra stands in the doorway, looks at us all.

—It's ready, she finally says, and turns, and we all file after her into the kitchen, then wait uncertainly at the table until Dave gives Danny a shove toward the chair closest to me, and we all sit. In the middle of the table is a large platter, holding a big black lumpy piece of meat. Danny looks at it, disappointed; he has remembered the steak. Dave watches him stare at the meat.

—What? Dave finally says, and Danny looks away.

—Nothing, he says. —This looks great.

—I hope you like pot roast, Myra says. She turns from the sink, holding up a bowl in each hand; her eyes droop under the startling arch of her brows, and she sways slightly from side to side. Behind her on the counter, our cocktail glasses are all empty but for a few pieces of fruit in the bottom and pink foam clinging to the sides. The little plastic monkeys are lined up in a row next to the glasses; they appear to be watching us. I remind myself to ask for my monkey before I leave. Myra sets the bowls on the table, then takes her seat. Sitting so close to her, I can see tiny fine lines in the delicate skin under her eyes, but the rest of her skin is stretched tightly over the bones, and when she turns to serve Danny, I see the scars behind her ears, not quite covered by her hair. They are long and lumpy, not the neat little incisions of a first-rate plastic surgery.

One of my sister's magazines had a feature on face-lifts, showing, step-by-step, the whole process in full-page photographs. First there was the woman just before the operation; then three or four pictures from the operation itself, showing the cutting and stretching and removing of skin; then the woman just after, scarred and bruised and bloody; and, finally, the finished product, the healed, altered face.

My sister put all the pictures on the wall right next to her bed; I used to see her study them sometimes at night when she thought I was sleeping. She kneeled on her bed and stared closely at the pictures from the operation, running her finger down her face in the patterns made by the incisions in the photographs. When Myra turns and sees my eyes on her, she quickly brings her hand to her face, and smoothes her hair down over the scars behind her ears. She turns from me.

—Dave, she says. —The wine, and Dave gets a bottle of wine from the counter, twists off the cap, and fills the tumblers at each of our places. We all sit a moment, looking at our full plates of food.

Live girls

This is not how we ate meals in my house. At my house, we ate our meals from trays in front of the television. We stood in the kitchen with our trays while my mother put food on them, and then we carried the trays into the living room. My father could eat a whole tray full of food without once taking his eyes from the television, while my mother sat by, watching with un-masked disgust. After a while, all she cooked were frozen TV dinners—if he was going to pay so little attention to what he ate, she said, she could hardly see the point of spending a lot of time cooking it. As for me, I suppose I could have carried my tray through the living room and kept right on walking out of the house and into the street, and eaten my meals there. But I always joined them.

My sister, after a while, stopped bothering to eat with us at all, which was something of a relief, since all she did was mash her food into a big pile, then lean over her tray and stare angrily at my parents. When she withdrew permanently to her own room, I took her meals to her, laying her tray outside her door, the way one would feed a prisoner, or an animal at the zoo. I always knocked to let her know it was there, and at first I used to wait for her to open her door, but when she'd see me there, she'd just snatch something quickly from the tray and slam the door. Sometimes I'd walk away, clomping my feet loudly, then creep silently back and linger at her door, breathless, listening. Some-times I was sure I could hear her chew, and I would close my eyes and feel her throat move as she swallowed. I had been used to seeing her every day, and now she was gone. Sometimes I could not remember what she looked like.

In the mornings her tray was always back out in the hall; I never heard her put it there, and I used to imagine that sometime in the middle of the night, when we were all sleeping, she would emerge from her room and roam around the house, watching television, perhaps, or looking out the windows into the front yard. She came back to our room some nights, I was sure of it;

I dreamed of her standing at my bed while I slept, reaching to touch my face, watching over me. It seemed too real not to be true.

Next to me, Danny chews; his mouth is closed and his breathing is intense, heavy. He is enjoying his food. He will always enjoy his food. He breathes and chews and eats like a machine; first he eats his meat, all of it, then his potatoes, all of them, and turns at last to his beans.

Myra clears her throat. —Well, she says to Danny. —I suppose Irma knows you're here?

Danny stops chewing and nods, but Myra stares at him, waiting, and he swallows the food in his mouth, then stares down at his plate.

—Jesus Christ, Dave says. He tosses his fork on his plate and looks at me.

—Her sister, he says. —They hate each other.

—I beg your pardon, Myra says. —I do not hate my sister. I love my sister dearly. I love *all* of my sisters dearly.

This last is directed at Dave and clearly with some sort of pointed message; the look they exchange makes even Danny put down his fork. I stand and ask directions to the bathroom. Dave does not break his gaze with Myra, but points in the direction of the living room, and I leave, then follow a long hallway down to the only open door. Next to the door is a little table of photographs; the largest is a picture of Dave and a woman. It takes me a moment to recognize the woman as Myra. It's a picture that could be taken years from now, so much older does she appear; her face is lined with wrinkles, her eyes puffy and swollen, and her hair is almost completely gray, whereas now it is a kind of strawberry blond.

Next to that is a picture of four people in a desert. Dave is in the foreground, smiling down at a woman who resembles Myra, but Myra is a short distance away watching them. Next to her is a man leaning down to examine something on the ground.

As I pick up the picture, I feel someone behind me, and I turn. Dave is standing at the end of the hallway watching me.

—I thought maybe you got lost, he says. The light is behind him, and I can't see the expression on his face.

—I was just looking at your pictures, I say, and he walks down the hall toward me.

—This is nice, I say, holding out the picture of the two couples. He nods. —That was in Arizona. He points at the man. —That's Myra's husband, he says. —Before me.

—Oh, I say. —Who's the woman?

He pauses, looking down at the picture. —My wife, he says. —Before Myra. He glances behind him, toward the kitchen.

—They look a lot alike, I say, and he stares down at the picture; his face says nothing at all.

—I guess, he finally says, then walks away. I look back at the picture. Dave is smiling down into the face of a woman he would one day kill, and Myra is watching. There is no clue in her face as to what she wants; there is no clue in anyone's face. Dave is holding a cowboy hat in his hand. It seems impossible that he could ever have worn a cowboy hat. It seems impossible that he could have killed the woman he is smiling at, and it seems impossible that he could have married her sister. It seems impossible, and I put the picture back on the table and go into the bathroom.

The bathroom is full of cats: there are cats printed on the towels, and tiny soaps in the shape of cats; there are cats on the shower curtain, and a row of little plastic cats on the shelf above the mirror.

—I guess you like cats, I say when I come back to the table. The tension is not much broken, and Myra seems not to have touched her food, though her wineglass is empty.

—Yes, she says, without much enthusiasm. She is looking at Dave, bent over his plate.

—Me too, I say. —I love cats. I have one of my own.

I put a hard little potato in my mouth and smile around the table, but no one is paying attention but Danny.

—Her name is Debbie, I add. I can feel Danny looking at me.

—Debbie, he repeats softly, puzzled.

Myra sighs. —I'd like to have a pet, she says wistfully. —But Dave hates them. And, she adds pointedly, —cats are *awfully* fragile. So many things can happen to them.

Dave takes a breath and starts to say something, then puts a piece of meat in his mouth instead.

—What about Blackie? I say, and Myra looks at me.

—What? she says.

—Blackie. Isn't Blackie a pet?

—Blackie, she says. —Don't get me started on Blackie.

—Blackie? Danny says.

—Christ, says Dave. —The dog. He glares at Danny, and Danny looks down at the little pools of brown and green juice on his plate.

—Blackie, Myra repeats bitterly.

We all sit quietly a moment, while outside Blackie paces over the small circle of dirt where he will spend his life.

Finally, Myra holds out her hand for Danny's plate, which he gives her, and she cuts him a piece of meat that covers nearly the whole plate. She smiles as he takes a bite.

—You probably don't get many good home-cooked meals like this, she says, and Danny looks at her.

—Irma never was much of a cook, she adds, and Danny swallows, then looks down at the meat on his plate as if he is debating. Finally, he cuts another bite, and resumes eating. He eats unself-consciously, though the rest of us have already finished, and Myra watches every bite. I wonder where she was when Dave killed his first wife, if she was waiting for it to happen, if she stood there in that desert watching him, wanting the man who loved her sister to be hers, while the man who had chosen her bent away from her to examine something on the ground—an insect, or a stone, or a grain of sand. And now what she wanted is hers: Dave, this life. And there is Blackie too, and Danny, and now, apparently, me.

When he finishes, Danny leans back and sighs, looks around. This is how our meals will end. We will have meat and potatoes, and a plate of bread in the corner of the table. Perhaps on Sunday we will eat with Danny's parents, and occasionally we will come here. This will be my life, and every day I will forget about any life I led before this one.

When Myra stands to clear the table, even I, who do not know her, can see that she is drunk. She holds the back of her chair as she collects plates, and she swallows the inch or two of wine left in Dave's glass before she puts it in the sink. She leans against the counter, then turns and focuses her eyes on Dave.

—Blackie? she says. —What happened to Blackie?

Dave rolls his eyes. —Nothing, he says. —He's in the yard.

—Something happened to him, she says. —Someone killed him.

Dave sighs, and looks off. —No, he says after a long while. —No one killed him. He's fine.

She nods driftily, then turns back to the sink, but when Dave stands, scraping his chair suddenly along the floor, she jerks and drops a glass, which shatters in the sink. For a moment nothing happens, then Dave lowers himself carefully back into his chair. Myra does not turn, but stares down into the sink, and the look Dave levels at her back is hard to read; it is the look of a man who killed his wife, and who must be daily accused of some murder or other, even those that have not even occurred. After he scoots his chair back to the table, Myra begins picking out pieces of glass from the sink, setting them carefully on the counter. She sucks in her breath suddenly, and stops; when she turns, she holds up her palm. A thin line of blood runs down her hand, from her finger to her wrist, and she stares at Dave.

—Well, I say, standing. —I'm all in.

Dave stands too, and Myra lowers her arm. Only Danny stays seated; he looks up at me, then realizes suddenly that I am leaving, and he stands too, smiling uncertainly around at everyone.

Dave walks us to the door and when I turn to say goodbye to him, Myra has moved back to the table, her plastic face lit up under the bright kitchen light; her hand is at her face, pressing against the edge of her mouth, as if to force it into some other shape. The line of blood has reached her elbow.

—Okay, Dave says. He pushes us gently out onto the front step, then follows us and closes the door behind him.

—Okay, he says again. —See you tomorrow, I guess.

—Okay, I say, and at the noise of my unfamiliar voice, Blackie lets out a little sound, something between a yelp and a growl; he silences himself immediately, and then there is nothing but the jingle of his chain.

As we cross the lawn, Danny stops to re-examine the plastic squirrels in the yard, and I go to wait in his car; Dave is still on the doorstep, looking out, but not at us. All there is to see are other houses, all of them just like his. Most of them are lit and inside people are moving around: families sitting to dinner or going over homework or planning the next day. Nowhere do I see a girl like I was; nowhere do I see a girl like my sister.

Danny joins me in the car, and as we pull away, he waves at Dave, who does not wave back. Danny sighs.

—I liked those drinks, he says, and I nod. I have forgotten to take the monkey from my glass; I was planning to hang it by its tail from the edge of my bedpost, and when I woke up, there it would be, every morning, like a pet, looking down at me with tiny plastic monkey eyes.

—They were really good, he says. He smells of alcohol, and I can see that he is not used to drinking.

Live girls

. . .

He talks as he drives, in a kind of dreamy monotone, as though
he is not talking to anyone at all, just talking. He likes to make
things, he says, he likes to carve them out of wood; all kinds of
things—tables and shelves and little statues. He likes those squirrels in Dave's yard, he says; he likes yards, and doing yard work.
His voice is pleasant and drowsy and when he turns to look at me
every now and then, his eyes are milky in the dim light. Our yard
will be beautiful, full of trees and grass and flowers, and birds
will come from everywhere to perch in our trees and rest on the
little wooden statues Danny carves; he will make small wooden
squirrels that put Dave's to shame; they will seem so real that
living squirrels will come to play among them. Our children will
watch them from their windows. We will live like this forever.

When we reach the building Danny thinks is mine, Danny cuts
his lights and engine, then closes his eyes and turns, but even as
he reaches toward me, I am out of the car. I have the door
closed by the time he opens his eyes, and he stares at me a moment, startled, as I say good night. He does not restart his car
until I reach the door of the building, and waits until I've gone
inside the vestibule before he turns on his lights.
I wave at him through the glass outer door, but all I can see is
his face in shadows, turned to watch me. The vestibule smells
of mildew; a damp stack of ad circulars molds in the corner,
and flyers litter the floor; from one flyer a child looks up at me,
asking if I have seen her. Her face is darkened with the scuff
marks of shoes. Outside, Danny is still waiting, watching me
from his car, and I make a show of fumbling for keys. I hold up
my key to the door to show him, but still he waits, and so I stand
in front of the little row of mailboxes and pretend to unlock
one, though all the locks have sprung and every box is open. I
pull out a stack of mail, then lean back against the wall, sorting
through it. Finally, Danny pulls slowly off.

The mail is mostly junk, a few bills. I put it all back in the box except for one envelope that reads: *Have You Been Lonely Too Long?* It is addressed to Resident, and I put it in my pocket. As I walk to the Hygienic, it feels as if all the cars that pass are slowing to watch me, then speed up and drive away. Perhaps they take me for a hooker.

I stop on the sidewalk outside the Hygienic. I have not seen Jerome for a few days, not since I saw him with the sailors, but he is here now, sitting at the counter next to Eric, their backs to me. Jerome turns to Eric, and leans sideways, his head on Eric's shoulder, but Eric jerks away, so that Jerome has to grab onto the counter to keep his balance. Eric turns on his stool and looks around the room, then out the window. When he sees me, he smiles, opens his mouth, waggles his tongue, and Jerome turns to see who it is he is looking at. Even at this distance, I can see the marks of a beating on Jerome's face—ugly blue and red patches on his cheek, swollen dark skin around his lip and eye. Eric grins and rises from his stool, but I turn and head toward my hotel. A big pale car slows as it passes; it is like Danny's car, but I cannot see the face of the driver; he cuts his lights as he turns the corner.

Back in my room, back on my bed, and next door the men on the radio have got someone by the throat. His name is Ed; he calls often, almost every night. The radio hosts hate him; they think he asks stupid questions.

—So, Ed, one of them says. —You must be a pretty lonely guy.
—I guess so, Ed says.
—Hey, Ed, says the other. —You married?
—No, Ed says.
—Got a girlfriend?
—Not really, Ed says.
—Ohhhhkay, they say. —How about a pet? A dog?
—No.

Live girls

—Cat?

—No.

—Fish! they say, chortling. —Turtle!

—No, Ed says, —I–but they cut him off.

—Ed, they say, very serious now. —Do you have any plants?

—No, Ed says patiently, —but I was wondering what you guys thought the Yankees might do next season.

There is a silence, then one sighs. —Gee, he says, suddenly thoughtful. —Gee, Ed, I dunno. That's really a tough one, you know, Ed, considering the season only ended a month or two ago. It's really hard to say.

—Yeah, says Ed, —I thought so, because–but they cut him off again.

—Ed, they say, —we gotta go. We gotta lotta calls coming in.

—Oh, Ed says. —Well, yeah, I gotta go too; but before he has finished, they cut the connection.

—Jesus, one of them says. —Next call?

I roll over on my side and pull out the envelope I took from the apartment building. Inside is a letter and a form. *Dear Single,* the letter begins. *Tired of the Dating Scene?* it asks, and I nod, though I have never really dated. *Tired of being alone?* I nod. *Tired of not meeting enough quality people?*

"Quality people" is the kind of phrase Dave might use to describe the people he wants to attract to his theater, or the kind of men he thinks I should be spending time with.

I turn to the form, which is a questionnaire divided into two sections: one about me and one about what it calls my ideal partner. The questions about me are pretty straightforward–age, income, interests, and so on. I tell the truth about my age, but give myself a higher income and a better education. The list of interests includes several activities: dancing, reading, movies, sports, nature. I check them all, then move to a question about my primary social goal. Marriage is first, then a steady relationship, then dating. I leave it blank. The last question asks if I plan to move within the next six months. I circle yes, then scratch it out and circle no, then scratch out the whole question and look back over my answers.

I seem to be the kind of person someone might want to go out with—a woman with many interests and many options. I turn to the second section, and a long list of questions about my potential mate: his appearance, habits, interests, and so on. Every question has a list of options, ranging from Very Important to Does Not Matter, including the question about his marital status. The first question is about his income. Does Not Matter, I check. This is not how my sister would have answered this question. The man she married, she used to tell me, would be rich, and he would love her so much it would kill him. At their wedding she would wear a long white veil made of pearls, and as she walked down the aisle, we would hold our breaths at her beauty, then gasp in awe and delight when he lifted her veil to kiss her. And I, I would be in the back row, she always added, holding little bags of rice and rose petals to hand out to the guests. This always seemed possible when she talked about it, and I used to imagine my parents sitting proudly in the front row, surrounded by a churchful of friends and family who had never before come forward to know us, while I would finally be left alone, spinsterish, standing in a circle of rose petals, watching my sister leave me.

She picked out her wedding dress when she was twelve, from a bridal magazine she'd got. It covered the whole body, even the neck and most of the hands. If she died before she married, she told me once, I had to make sure they got her this dress and buried her in it. She kept the picture tacked up to the head of her bed; while we shared a room, it was the only picture she never changed.

Down the hall the toilet flushes, then again, and again, and several times more. I once eavesdropped on some cops at the Hygienic who were enthralling some old men with a story about a recent incident, which is what they call all murders; in this case a man killed his wife, then tried to flush her, piece by piece, down the toilet. One of the cops laughed and said he might have gotten away with it if he'd had better plumbing. They all chuckled and looked at me.

Debbie's door opens and closes. —Debbie, the man says, —Debbie, look. Tuna.

I get up and put my ear against the wall.

—Tuna, he says again. His voice is false and bright. —You love tuna. He hums a little song I recognize from an old cat-food commercial on television, but it trails off after a few bars, and his voice goes melancholy again, pleading for her to eat. After a while he is silent, and I go to the bathroom. It smells of fish. Tiny fish bones cling to the sides of the sink, glittering under a sheen of yellowish oil. I run water over it, but it only spreads oil across the porcelain, so I wash my face, which just adds to the mess. I wipe it all up as best as I can with a wad of toilet paper, then flush it down the toilet.

Back in my room, I smell of fish; my hair and hands and skin all smell of it, and I can taste it in the back of my throat. I look back over the questionnaire; I have answered only one question on my potential mate so far, but I decide to leave it until tomorrow. *This will make you happy at last,* the letter promises. I fold it all up and drop it under my bed. This will make me happy at last, I think.

—Debbie, the man croons next door.

—Debbie, I whisper, —this will make us happy at last. She drinks her water.

The man watches her. They will be here forever.

I close my eyes and try to imagine the man I will meet from the dating service. He will be handsome; he will be tall; he will be from a good family, but when I close my eyes, it is Danny's face that appears there. He is waiting for me; he is still circling the building where he thinks I live. Someday I will learn to love him; we will live together in a little house, among the things he has carved us out of wood, the shelves and cabinets and tables, and at night we will sleep on wooden sheets and pillows. I will wake to the touch of his wooden hand on my face. Outside, the wooden grass grows stiff and sharp. Our yard is full of little pets, dogs and cats that Danny has carved of wood, and playing cautiously among them are the tiny children he has made. Their little wooden legs creak in the damp air.

In the distance my sister watches, her face hidden behind a wooden veil; she watches as Danny carves the face of our youngest daughter. She is waiting for the knife to slip. In the distance is the sound of pigeons, trapped inside the trees. I listen to the noise of their wings, beating over and over against the dry bark.

Danny is standing behind the counter when I come to work. He is wearing a tiny brown bow tie. His collar is too tight around his neck; it squeezes his throat, and his head swells up over the tie like a beefy balloon. Dave is behind him, dumping popcorn into the machine.

Dave nods at me as I pass them to get to my bubble. A travel brochure pokes up from the pocket of his shirt. *Visit Arizona,* it says.

—Okay, he says to Danny. He points at the popcorn machine.
—Popcorn, he says, then points to the little stack of paper bags. —Bags. Okay?

Danny picks up one of the bags, and though it is the kind of bag he has been eating his popcorn from since he started coming here, he looks disappointed.

—Just these brown ones? he says, and Dave rolls his eyes, but I know he is sensitive on this point; there was a time, when I first came, that we had red-and-white striped bags, with little elephants printed on the front. They disappeared with Patty, and since then we have had only the brown ones.

—Look, Dave says. —When you're in charge, you can have any kind of bags you want, but for now, use these. Okay?

—That machine's still broken, I say from my bubble, and Dave gives me an annoyed look.

—It's not broken, he snaps to Danny, but Danny stares at the machine as if it's a bomb about to go off. Dave sighs. —Watch, he says, with exaggerated patience. He pops open one of the bags, fills it with popcorn, and hands it to Danny.

—Just like that, he says. —Just scoop it in. Okay?

Danny nods and Dave says okay again, then goes to his office. As I sell tickets, I hear the noise of scooping behind me; when I turn, Danny has lined up several bags of popcorn on top of the counter. Grease is already seeping through the paper in dark blots. Danny watches disconsolately as the last customer enters the theater. He looks over at me.

—No one bought any, he says.

—Don't worry, I tell him. —It takes a while.

He nods. —Thanks, he says, then edges closer to my bubble.

—I'm not really used to working with the public, he says. I nod.

—Who is? I say, and he gazes off thoughtfully a moment, considering.

—Well, he begins, but I cut him off.

—I guess you don't work with the public much at your job, I say, and he shakes his head.

—No, he says. —Just, you know, pests.

—Pigeons, I say, and he nods. He looks past me, at the pictures of the woman from the cave, taped to my bubble.

—Wow, he says. —Who's that?

—My sister, I say. —Catherine. She lives in Arizona.

—Oh, he says. —She's pretty.

I nod, and his gaze shifts to outside the bubble. I turn. Eric is there, with a different woman tonight; she stares off down the street while Eric buys the tickets.

—Hey, doll, he says to me. When I try to take his money, he keeps his hand on it a moment, holding it down so I have to tug.
—You're a doll, he says. —I could just eat you up.
He turns to the woman. —Hey, he says, —ain't she a doll? Couldn't you just eat her right up?
The woman glances at me. —Yeah, she says, then goes back to staring off down the street until Eric pulls her inside.

Danny stands alertly at the candy counter, but Eric just breezes past.
—Hiya, sport, he says to Danny. —Nice tie.
Danny watches them walk inside. —Hiya, sport, he repeats softly.
He looks down at the candy, then crouches to peer inside.
—There's not much candy here, he says.
—No, I say. —Open one. He stands up quickly and backs away from the candy counter.
—No, I say, —really. It's okay. He gazes at me a moment, then steps forward and gingerly removes a box of Dots from its stack. Just as he opens it, Dave comes downstairs from the projection room.
—Hey, he barks at Danny. —Get away from that.
Danny closes the box up quickly and puts it back, then moves far away from the counter; he leans against the popcorn machine, watching Dave go into his office, then suddenly jerks forward as he feels the heat on his back. His shirt is stuck to his skin in a greasy circle on his back; he looks over his shoulder to try to see it, and plucks the shirt away from his skin, then gives me a quick resentful look.

He spends the evening far from the candy counter, and does not approach my bubble again, but I can feel his eyes on me. I want to sit completely still. I want to draw a curtain between us. Outside, it is sleety and cold. The woman from the cave looks down at me. She said that she thought about weather all the time at first when she was underground, but after a while she forgot what weather was. Sometimes she would lie on her bed and think: Rain, but she could not remember what rain was, what it felt like on her skin. The sun became something she could hardly believe was even real, and after a while, she wrote, light itself began to confuse her. Weeks went by in which she would never turn the lights out in her little room; then suddenly there would be days where she could stand nothing but darkness, and she would not turn the lights on, lying on her bed for days, unable to see a thing—not the walls, or the floor, or even her own hand in front of her face.

As the last crowd of the night straggles out, Danny and Dave and I stand at the doors, watching the parade of lowlife outside. Dave has one hand on my back, one on Danny's. A little band of drag queens comes down the sidewalk, Jerome bringing up the rear in a big yellow boa. He waves at me.

—Yoo-hoo, he calls out. —Hi, honey. One of his heels is wobbly, and his stocking is run from his ankle all the way to his thigh. His face is streaked with pancake a shade or two lighter than his skin, so that his face and neck are two different colors; a bruise blossoms on his jaw, like a purple flower unfolding under dirty snow.

—Freak, Dave mutters, and Danny brightens.

—Yeah, he says. —Freak.

Before the group has got out of sight, Danny steps forward to the glass doors. —Freak, he yells. —Freak. Jerome startles at the sound, like a cat twitching its ears at the sound of his name, but he does not turn. Dave steps forward to pull Danny from the doors.

—Hey, he says. —Hey, and Danny looks surprised at the reproach. He lowers his head.

—Well, he says, looking out the doors, —he is a freak.

My back feels chilly and exposed where Dave's hand was, and I brush past them to leave. Good night, I say, without looking back. A cold light drizzle is just beginning to fall and ahead of me the transvestites let out little shrieks at the rain. Jerome's boa has already begun to droop. I follow behind them, but when they see a little pack of sailors on the other side of the street, they cross over to talk to them, and I head home.

—Fuck you, someone says down in the alley outside my room, and someone else replies, —No, fuck you. —Go home, the first voice says, and the second answers, —You go home. After a while there is the sound of a splash; someone has thrown water on them and they go away.

—Debbie, the man says, —Debbie, eat; Debbie, wake up; Debbie, talk to me. I drift to sleep, surface awake. I sleep in my clothes; I don't like the feel of the sheets against my skin.

Freak, someone says, and I jerk awake, but it is just Danny. I am dreaming, I tell myself, this is a dream. Freak, Danny says, and he reaches out to me, he pulls me into our little wooden house. There is a room for my sister, he tells me; she can live here with us. Our lips meet, our wooden tongues touch in a kiss. The dry space between us shudders; I can hear my sister beat her wings against the walls of her room.

Days pool, collecting like water. Outside, men pass, their eyes tearing in the chill wind, and behind me, Danny lines up bags of popcorn like little rows of soldiers. As he chews, he watches me and plans our life together, wondering about the faces of our children, trying to decide whose faces he will carve theirs to resemble. They will be strong and sturdy like him, and at night when we have put them down to sleep, he will reach for me with his huge wooden hands, and then he will lie on top of me like a wooden box.

In his office, Dave sits at his desk, brochures falling like ashes around him. He drops his cigarettes on the carpet as he stares at the walls. Heat rises; he is dreaming of the desert. He is dreaming of his wife. There must be some way he could not have killed her.

Every day, the bruises on Jerome's face are covered by new ones, bruises on bruises, like autumn leaves: purple over red over yellow. —Girl, he says. —Girl, I got to change my life, and, alone in my room, spiders run through the cave of my chest. I can feel them tremble with every beat of my heart. My sister watches from the trees; she is waiting for me. She holds out her hand. *Save me,* she whispers, and the words are like feathers falling on my face. *Save me.*

Christmas is approaching; every now and then, I see a tree tied to a car, and even Dave has given in to the spirit with a ratty old wreath in the front of my booth. The current movie has a holiday theme, and the woman in the poster in front wears a Santa cap; little elves climb over her legs and breasts, their faces split by lecherous little elf grins. At the college, the girls wait for Christmas in a breathless frenzy of devotion; the hill hums with their spirit as they look down at us, we who have not been saved. Jesus, they breathe, Jesus saves.

Sleet splatters in through my window. I start another letter to my parents. I have started so many letters to them, but I have not mailed one since my sister died. *I have changed my plans,* I write, *I am going to Arizona for Christmas. Phoenix. My friends are all going to a ranch there in the desert, owned by one of their fathers, and they have invited me to come along.* A ranch, my sister would think; she would imagine herself perched on a large golden horse, surrounded by boys. They would worship her. *And I will have a horse named Tony,* I add to my letter. *I will ride him all day, and at night he will stand outside my window while I sleep.* I put down my pen. Tony, I think. This is somehow familiar to me, but I have never touched a horse. I close my eyes. Something is moving inside me somewhere, moving.

Live girls

. . .

On my way to work, I stop at a grocery store to buy a Christmas card. Cards are all we exchange for the holidays; the exchange of presents was always difficult for us, especially at Christmas—my sister and I would open our boxes of socks and pencils and useful things while my mother stared down, not bothering to mask her disappointment at whatever kitchen utensil or cleaning apparatus my father had gotten her. There was a time when I bought presents for my sister, the kinds of junky colorful things that children are attracted to—but I always saw them turn up much later in the possession of some other child, someone whose friendship she had bought for an hour or so with the lure of a barrette in the shape of a pony, or a pen that could write in different colors. I once saw a ball I had given her bouncing down the street in and out of the hand of a boy I watched a few years later follow my sister down an alley; I watched his hands move over her body that day, just as I had watched him bounce the ball in the bright afternoon.

There are plenty of Christmas cards, and I go through most of them before I find one with the right message: *Season's greetings*, it says. On the front, a cat sits next to a Christmas tree, looking down at a little stack of presents in its food bowl.

All the while I have been looking over cards, a partially filled grocery cart has been left next to me. It holds food for a party—potato chips, little tubs of dip, a six-pack of beer, several large bottles of soda. No one has come near it since I have been here, and I look around, then drop my card into the front of the basket and push it away.

I wheel around the store for a while before I stop. I am like everyone else, I think; I am having a party. I will invite Jerome, and Dave. Danny. I add to my basket a large bag of popcorn, a can of wax beans, some cottage cheese. A few women stand in front of the meat section, looking down over the selection, and

I join them. Danny will want meat for our meals, and plenty of it. Behind the glass, a man in a butcher's apron saws patiently at a big hunk of something on a table. His apron is splattered with blood, and after a while he severs what looks like a leg from the piece of meat. He throws it into a large garbage can behind him. When he looks up and sees me watching him, he smiles and brings his cleaver to his cap in a kind of salute. I turn and push my cart away. The pet-food aisle has rows and rows of cat food; I wonder if Debbie's owner has tried them all. As I look over the different brands, I feel a child beside me, reaching up for a box of dog biscuits. I almost offer to lift her up when I realize it is a woman, a dwarf. She looks at me, and I look quickly back at the cat food.

—Excuse me, she says. —Can you hand me that? She points to a box of dog biscuits. I hand them to her, and she puts them in the basket she carries, then moves to the other side of me, looking up at the cat food. After a while, she becomes aware of me watching her, and turns to face me. I smile, but she just stares back.

—I was just wondering what kind you were going to get, I say.

—My cat is very picky.

She looks at me a long moment, then points at a stack of cans out of her reach. —That's good, she says. —My cat likes that.

I pile several cans of it into my cart, and wheel off, pushing up and down a few aisles without adding anything. There is so much food here, doughnuts and bread and ice cream and cans of things. It occurs to me that I do not know what my sister liked to eat, what kinds of foods were her favorite. Sometimes she ate what she was given and sometimes she did not, but there was no sense to it. One night she might eat nothing but the dessert from her TV dinner, and the next she might ignore it completely and eat only the vegetables. I do not remember what she liked to eat; I do not remember her favorite color, or what outfits she liked to wear as a child.

At some point, walking up and down aisles, I realize I am following the dwarf. All the people she passes avert their eyes, then turn quickly to watch her; they always look in her basket. As I follow, I add things to my cart; sometimes I add something she herself has chosen and sometimes I add things at random, then follow on, until we are in the produce section at the far end of the store. She is standing in front of a large pile of oranges; she reaches up for one, and several tumble down onto the ground around her. People turn to look at her, then quickly look away. I look down at my cart. It is packed full of food, all kinds of food, food I don't even know what to do with—big cans of lard, loaves of frozen bread, a bag of flour. I wheel the cart into a corner by some vegetables, and take one of the cans of cat food from the top, then walk away, and pretend to inspect the potatoes. The dwarf is gone. Oranges roll across the floor. No one seems to notice me, and I take my cat food to the checkout area; there is a line at every stand, and after a moment I put the cat food in my pocket and leave the store. No one stops me. The can bumps against my side in the pocket of my coat, and it is not until I am at the theater that I remember the Christmas card, buried under all that food.

Eric is back at the theater. While the woman he has brought with him goes to the bathroom, he stops to chat with Danny. He leans back against the counter, and together they watch the sparse crowd trickle in. Eric shakes his head.
—Lame crowd, he says, and Danny nods.
—Lame crowd, Danny repeats.
Eric glances at the bags of popcorn Danny has already lined up on the counter, then reaches out and takes a handful from the top of one. Danny looks alarmed, and Eric looks at me while he chews.
—You know what you need? he asks, and Danny shakes his head. Eric looks at him. —I'll tell you, he says. —You need live

girls. He nods, looking around the lobby. —Yeah, he says. —Two shows a night? You'd clean up. Danny stares at him, and Eric takes another handful of popcorn from the top of a different bag. —Listen, he says. —This shit–he waves at the theater–you can rent this shit in any grocery store. You want something to get them sailors in here, them young guys. Not these lame old geezers.

—Geezers, Danny says. He nods. —Geezers, he says again.

—Look, Eric says. —You even seen this shit? Danny shakes his head.

—Come on, Eric says. —You ain't even watched it?

—No, Danny says.

—Man, Eric says. —Come on. You got to see the product. Hey, he says, —I'm a entrepreneur. Trust me.

The woman he has brought comes out of the bathroom and goes to wait for him by the theater doors. Eric stares at her, then finally grabs another handful of popcorn and saunters over to join her.

—See ya, he says to Danny over his shoulder. —Sport.

Dave comes down from the projection booth and heads straight for his office without even a glance at us. He sits at his desk and picks up a brochure. He stares straight ahead at the wall as he turns the pages. Danny carefully tops off each bag of popcorn that Eric ate from, and straightens the whole row, then stands and stares out at the lobby. Suddenly he turns and walks quickly into the theater without looking back at me.

The woman from the cave looks through me. She said that there were days when she found herself in the middle of some chore, like brushing her teeth, and she would have to stop, suddenly unsure whether she had just begun the task or had been at it for hours.

When I hear Danny come out of the theater, I keep my back to him, but I can hear him behind me, emptying all the bags of popcorn into the machine, then refilling and emptying them over and over.

When the show ends, Eric leaves his date in the middle of the lobby and comes over to the counter. Danny glances nervously at the bags of popcorn he's lined up, but Eric ignores them. He lights a cigarette and drops the match on the floor.

—See what I mean? he says. —This shit's tired. He looks to either side, then leans forward toward Danny as if he is about to level with him.

—Live girls, he says. —Think about it. He walks away, then stops and turns. —Guy like you, he says, —you could go a long way. He grins. —See ya, sport, he adds with a little salute that sends cigarette ash onto the rug. Danny looks pleased as Eric walks away.

Dave has been watching this exchange from the bottom of the stairs, and as Eric joins his date, Dave comes to the counter.

—Listen, he says to Danny. —You don't want to be associating with that lowlife.

Together they watch Eric leave; as he passes my bubble, he waggles his tongue at me, almost as an afterthought.

—He's an entrepreneur, Danny says, and Dave snorts.

—Entrepreneur, Dave says, and shakes his head, turning to his office.

—He was saying we should get live girls, Danny says, and Dave stops.

—He says we'd clean up, Danny says, and Dave looks at him a moment, interested, then shrugs.

—Whatever, he says, then goes back to his office. Danny turns and sees me watching. He nods.

—Live girls, he says. —It's something to think about.

I turn away. I can hear him chewing popcorn. I can feel him watching me. He is thinking of live girls. He will come home at night with the scent of live girls on his skin. When I turn and look at him, he gazes back at me, chewing; he looks at me as if I am not here to look back at him.

When the last show ends, Dave comes out to the lobby. Outside, a hustler, a kid maybe fourteen or fifteen, leans against a street sign in front of the theater, watching the faces of the men as they leave; finally one walks over to him, and the hustler leans forward, puts the man's hand on his crotch, and closes his eyes. Dave pushes the door open.

—Hey, he barks. —Take it to a motel. The boy laughs and the two cross the street to the bench by the bus stop. Dave sighs.

—I don't need this, he says, more to himself than to me, though I am only a few feet away. He shakes his head. —I ought to move to Phoenix. He watches as the man bends down and unzips the boy's pants; the boy puts his head back. Dave drops his cigarette and watches it burn a small hole in the rug before he steps on it.

—I could be there by Christmas, he says. —Christmas in Arizona.

—What about the theater? I ask, and he looks at me a long moment, as if he is surprised to see me here. He shrugs.

—Danny can run it. What the hell. It beats killing birds.

He looks at Danny, who is flipping through a movie brochure. He stares at him for a while.

—Yeah, he says, and walks away nodding. —By Christmas. When Danny reaches the end of the brochure, he closes it, then flips back through it again, backward.

Jerome sits hunched over a bowl of wax beans. He glances up when I join him. He has caked blue eye shadow all around his eyes to hide the bruises, and it gives them a hidden, haunted look.

—Girl, he says. —What's going on?

—They're going to have live girls at the theater, I say, and he looks at me, hardly interested at all. He shakes his head.

—Live girls, he says. —Dead girls. Girls is girls. He pokes his fork through the beans, then pushes the bowl away.

—I'm a cow, he says, staring at the beans.

—No, I say. —No. You're beautiful.

—No, he says. —Look at me. He looks at our reflections in the mirror on the wall, and pinches the skin under his arm; there is nothing there, just tendons and stringy muscle.

—Oh, he says, —look, and he turns to look out the window. In the mirror, I see what he sees; it's Danny, standing outside on the sidewalk. He is holding a bag of popcorn.

—There's that boy of yours, Jerome says. He sighs. —What a dreamboat.

Danny looks in through the glass walls; our eyes meet in the mirror, and still he stares. He puts a handful of popcorn in his mouth and chews as he watches us.

—Oooh, Jerome says. —Popcorn. Absently he puts a wax bean in his mouth as he watches Danny, and for a moment they are chewing together, like two lovers breathing in sync, until Danny turns abruptly and walks away. Jerome stops chewing, then brings his napkin to his mouth and delicately removes the wax bean. He folds the napkin into a neat square and tucks it under his bowl.

As I walk home, every footstep behind me sounds like Danny, every car that passes seems to be his, and when I am home, lying on my bed, I know it is his breath I hear in the hallway against my door. I can hear him chew; I can hear the wooden click of his eyelashes as he blinks. A door opens and closes, and for a moment I am sure it is mine; I brace for the touch of a hand, then hear the rattle of a bag in the room next door.

—Look, Debbie, the man next door says. —Look what I brought you. Eat this.

—Debbie, I whisper, —eat that.

Outside in the alley, I hear the engine of Danny's car, then the slow glide of it down the street. The trunk is full of live girls. He is saving them. He is saving them all. I jerk awake to the hiss of electricity; outside my window, the Christmas lights have come on. A string of them hangs down past my window; one or two bulbs have broken out, and rain crackles as it hits the live sockets.

Danny only nods at me when I come into the theater. He keeps busy with his bags of popcorn, filling and refilling them, arranging and rearranging them. Dave goes upstairs to start the movie, and when he returns to his office, Danny gives his little row of popcorn one last look, then goes into the theater. He walks right past Dave's open door; I wait for Dave to notice him, to stop him and send him back to work, but he does not look up from his brochure. You don't want to watch that trash, is what he has always told me about the movies he shows, plot or no plot; that trash will ruin your mind.

The woman from the cave gazes out at me. I wonder what they did with her body when she died, if they buried her. I would think that the last thing she would have wanted was to go back underground. When my sister died, my mother called me at the school to tell me.

—Well, she said when I got on the line, —your sister died, and from the tone of her voice, she might have been saying your sister finally died, the way you would say the car or the dishwasher finally broke down. She sighed. —This is hard on us, she said. It was difficult to be in my parents' house without my sister. Her door was closed, and every time I passed it, I paused to listen for the sound of her breathing, of her moving around. It seemed impossible that she could die without making sure I went first. Even now, sometimes I think she must still be there in her room, sitting at her window as she waits for some boy to come along and save her, listening to the flutter of leaves against the glass, the stir of owls in the trees.

My roommate at the college believed that when we died, our bodies came with us to Heaven, regardless of how they were disposed of here on earth, and once we got there, we would be made whole again: the old became young, the crippled could walk, the blind see. That all went without saying, she said cheerily, and besides that, we would all be beautiful, with perfect skin and hair and teeth and bodies. It had to be that way, she told me, so that what was on the outside reflected the beautiful souls that God had chosen. She used to explain these things to me as if I were a child. It was what Jesus was for, she said, it was why he died. She herself had bad skin, subject to periodic angry breakouts that had already left what would clearly be permanent scars, tiny marks and pinholes all across her cheeks and forehead. They would be gone when she got to Heaven, shed and left behind like the skin of a snake.

As children, my sister and I were not especially encouraged to think about God or Heaven; to my sister, Heaven was primarily a place where she figured she would at last be free of the rest of us. Her real family was in Heaven, she said, and it was a family full of angels, with huge bright wings made of pearls. Her real sister was there too, and she was the most beautiful angel of all. They were waiting for her, and even if somehow I were allowed into Heaven, I would not be allowed to be with them. I used to imagine it sometimes: me, alone on a cloud of my own, watching them. I wondered if it ever grew dark in Heaven, so that I could inch closer to them, then sleep near them, in the dark shelter of their wings.

Across the street, a man steps up and down unsteadily from the curb to the street, up and down. He looks up and sees me, then wanders over, and stands right in front of my bubble. He has not shaved in a few days. His head is covered with a brown cap that has a little yellow ball on top. He stares at me.

—Well, he finally says, —look at you. He smiles. —Darlin'.

—Ticket? I say, and he stares at me as if he is considering.

—Darlin', he finally says. —Now why would I buy a ticket when I can look at you for free?

He puts his hands up on the glass and leans in close. I turn to look at Dave, but he is not watching me. He is staring at the wall in front of him. I get up just as the man's tongue is coming out of his mouth. Dave doesn't look up as I pass his office on the way to the bathroom. He has put a poster of Arizona up on the wall behind him; it is all sun and heat, rising behind his head like a wall of fire.

When I come out of the bathroom, the man is still at my window, leaning back against it now, his head to the glass.

No one notices when I slip into the theater. I spot Danny right away, sitting in a middle row, sitting up straight, his broad shoulders and head rising solidly out of his chair.

I take a seat near the back, on an aisle; one man a few rows in front of me turns at the squeak of my chair, stares a moment in the dark, then turns back to the movie. My seat feels grimy and the air is dense, damp; it feels like air that has already been breathed too much.

Every now and then, when the room brightens with the light from the screen, I can see Danny's face, staring up, his mouth slightly open, intent on the action; he looks like the kind of customer Dave would like to lure here: young and alert and interested. He could be watching art, so attentive does he appear. What he is watching is a woman walking down the street. It is Christmas; she passes two Santa Clauses and drops a dollar in their little kettle.

—Ho ho ho, one of them says as the woman heads across the street to a deserted parking lot. They turn their big Santa faces to each other, then cross the street after the woman. They catch up to her at her car. Danny's face is rapt. Light and color play across his face as he watches, and I think of his hands on me. One Santa stands to the side watching, while the other Santa lies on top of the woman, and then they switch. Her face is turned to the side, away from the audience. Her arms and legs look like parts of a doll, laid out on the ground, somehow separate, somehow waiting to be put together. It doesn't seem possible that she walked on those legs ever, that she used those hands to brush her hair, to eat, to button her blouse.

This is not real, I remind myself; this is only a movie. It is less real than a dream. The men run their hands along her legs and smile; they look at each other more often than they look at her. —Ho ho, they say. A man a few rows in front of me laughs, a short bark of sound. Danny turns his head at the sound, irritated, then quickly looks back up at the screen. This is not real, I tell myself as I walk up the aisle toward the exit. I turn at the sound of a slap from the screen, a cry, but they are not real. They are images on a screen, and they have nothing to do with me. Danny is leaning forward in his seat; he is watching as if all of this is real, as if it has something to do with him. One day he will wear a Santa suit to entertain his children. Ho ho, he will boom from behind his white beard, and his children will clap their tiny wooden hands. Ho ho, he will say; he will reach for me with his long wooden fingers.

The lobby is a sudden bright pool of light; the man is still outside, slumped against my bubble, his head turned to the side. Danny's keys sit on the little ledge near the popcorn machine, and I put them in my pocket, then go to stand at Dave's door. He is absorbed in his brochure. I cough, then say his name, but he keeps his head down, gazing at a picture of a desert, dotted all over with big green cactuses. I say his name again and he looks up. —I have an emergency, I say. —Tell Danny I had to borrow his car.

He gazes at me a long time, then nods. His eyes move back to the brochure before I have even turned away.

Danny's car is parked down the street. The man leaning against my bubble stirs as I pass him, then rouses.

—Hey, he says. He leans forward and makes a grab for me, then totters across the sidewalk.

—Hey, sister, he says, and I turn.

He trembles as he sways on his skinny legs; the little ball on top of his hat trembles, and his eyes are like the dead flat eyes of bugs and rats and things that live in cracks. He stares at me. For a moment I cannot move, and when I can, my legs are the legs of dolls, stiff and plastic, and my face is the face of a doll, a mask of stiff plastic features.

Nothing I have seems worth taking with me, so I leave everything but the box of my sister's things. Debbie's owner is just going into the bathroom with Debbie's bowl as I close my door, and when he sees me, he makes a peevish little face, then closes the bathroom door and locks it loudly. In his room, Debbie is hunched in her usual place, over the spot where her bowl normally sits. I lean my head in.

—Goodbye, Debbie, I say. Her ears flick.

—Debbie, I say again. She looks up at me with her tired yellow eyes and I am surprised by how suddenly and easily I am inside the room. It is just like mine except that the walls are covered with pictures of cats. Most of them are cut from magazines and newspapers, and there are pictures from calendars, cartoons, even ads for cat food. On the little table by the window is a stack of magazines, and several more pictures, and a little row of plastic cat figurines. There are so many cats that Debbie, hunched in the center of the floor, seems like the fake one, a pale imitation of the real thing. Her fur is ratty, and her ears are flat out at the sides, her elbows hunched up by her head. She is going to die there, right there in that spot.

I kneel down beside her. —Debbie, I whisper. She has a chemical smell, and when I pick her up, she does not protest. She weighs almost nothing at all; it is like picking up a hat or a pair of mittens, and I lay her inside my sister's box.

—Mother, I hear as I carry Debbie down the steps. —Mother. It is Ned, the old queen from my floor, talking to his mother on the phone; he is leaning back against the wall, his eyes closed. —Mother, he says again. —Mother, you have to listen. He opens his eyes as I pass, and looks at me; there is no expression on his face at all, as if I were just a piece of furniture moving past him. I am halfway down the stairs when I hear the bathroom door open.

The manager glances up at me as I walk through the lobby; his eyes go to the box, then to my face. This is how people skip out on the rent; they put their things into boxes, and then they walk right past him while he is reading the paper.

—Old clothes, I say. —For the homeless.

Debbie stirs uneasily inside the box; the manager watches us the whole way out.

Outside, as I unlock the doors to Danny's car, a rustle comes from the alley behind me. In the dark shadow of the big Dumpster there, the manager's wife is just visible, her purse dangling at her waist. Her face and eyes are masked by the darkness, but I can feel her watch me settle Debbie on the floor of the back seat, and put my sister's box in the trunk. She is there as I drive away; she will die there, standing in that alley watching people go by.

In Danny's big car, no one can see me—not the hookers or the drag queens or the men, going up and down the sidewalks and back again. It is like traveling through a world in a world of my own, and in this car I cannot be seen or heard or talked to or watched. I can go anywhere.

—Debbie, I say, —we can go anywhere.

She does not stir or make a sound; in the silence my voice is hollow. It is the same as being alone.

Live girls

. . .

We can go anywhere, but where I end up is the 7-Eleven where Jerome works.

He is still on duty, leaning back behind the counter, reading a magazine. He is wearing a baggy brown smock and his hair is pulled back in a ponytail. From here in the parking lot, he could be any young man who works at a convenience store. I've never seen him dressed as anything but a woman.

The store is empty but for a little group of boys playing a video game in the corner, and Jerome does not look up when I enter, or when I stand at the counter. He keeps his eyes intently focused on the magazine he is reading—it's a movie magazine, and he scans each page, then quickly turns to the next. A little red name tag on his smock reads *Jerry*. Under the flat bright store lights, and without makeup to cover them, the bruises on his face look fresh and ugly, big purple welts under his eye and along his jaw. He flips through the whole magazine before he lays it down with a put-upon sigh and looks at me. It takes a moment for recognition to register, and when it does, he does not look happy to see me.

—Girl, he says, —what are you doing here?

—I'm moving, I say. —Out of town.

—Oh, he says. —Well, you got to do what you got to do. Have a nice trip. He reaches for the movie magazine, then flips it open. I surprise even myself when I say, —I thought you might want to come.

He looks up at me. —With you? he says. I nod, and for just a moment I can see it, the three of us driving happily under a sunny sky, Debbie sleeping in Jerome's lap as he turns to me every now and then to read some bit of gossip from his magazine. He shakes his head.

—Honey, he says, —send me a postcard.

From the corner, the boys give out a little bunch of whoops over their video game and Jerome looks over at them. He sighs, then picks up his magazine. *Win a Trip to Hollywood* says an ad on the back, and underneath, a movie star smiles a dazzling smile of invitation.

—I'm going to Hollywood, I say, and Jerome lowers the magazine.

—Hollywood? he says. —What you going to do in Hollywood?

—My sister lives there, I say. He gazes at me a long time. His eyelashes are long and dark, and I wonder if they are natural or if he's risked wearing mascara on the job.

—I thought you was an orphan, he finally says, and I nod.

—I am. But I have a sister.

A boy comes into the store, and heads straight back to the group in the corner. Jerome watches him. Outside, traffic passes; soon a real customer may come in and I will lose him. Soon the movie will be ending at the theater, and Danny will come out to the lobby. He will wonder where I have gone. He will want his car.

—My sister's a talent agent, I say. —Her husband's a movie director.

—Uh-huh, Jerome says; his eyes follow one of the boys, who is walking aimlessly around the store; every now and then the boy glances up into the big convex mirror in the corner. It reflects him wherever he goes.

—I told him about you, I say. —He says he has a part for you. Jerome snaps his head back to look at me. —A part?

I nod. —In his new movie.

The effect of this on him is electrifying, and he stares at me, his face transformed.

—His new movie?

I nod again. —A big one. With big stars.

—Big stars, Jerome breathes, and once again I nod, as he looks around the store, turning his head slowly, as if it is a place he has already left and is trying to remember. His eyes stop at the boys by the video game, and while he watches them, I see the other boy slip a beer into his jacket. He turns and sees me watching, looks alarmed a moment, then winks.

Jerome finishes his survey of the room.

—Well, he says, —I can't just pick up and go.

The boy who has stolen the beer ambles out nonchalantly and Jerome watches him go. The boy hardly bothers to hide the beer, and pulls it out of his jacket before the door has even closed behind him.

—Can I? Jerome says, looking back at me, and what I see in his eyes is what he sees: himself, fifty feet tall, stared at by millions, the object of a thousand desires. It is his dream, and it is at war with what he knows: that people like me do not have sisters in Hollywood, and people like him do not become movie stars. People like us do not have lives like that; we have the kind of lives we already have and we would probably be better off if we just lived them.

Jerome searches my face, and I shrug.

—Well, I say, —I told him about you.

—You told him about me? he repeats, and I nod.

—But listen, I say, —I've got to go now. I turn to leave, and he says, —Wait.

I turn back and he gazes at me a moment, frozen, then looks nervously around the store. The boys are still absorbed in their game; there is no one else in the store, no one in the parking lot, no one pulled up to the gas tanks. Jerome takes a deep breath, then turns a key in the register and drops it into a drawer. I'm surprised by how seriously he takes his responsibility; the first time he mentioned this job, he looked dismayed to have let it slip that he worked at all, much less at a job like this. He comes around the corner with a nervous little giggle, and clutches my arm as we leave the store.

—Hollywood, here I come, he says, but stops short when I head for Danny's car.

—No, ma'am, he says. —I can't be going to Hollywood in this lame old piece of junk.

I look at Danny's car; it is beige and boxy, not at all glamorous or appetizing.

—It's all I have, I say. —We can trade it in when we get to Hollywood. He crosses his arms over his chest and shakes his head. I open my door.

—It belonged to a murderer, I say, and he perks up.

—No, he murmurs; his eyes go wide as he looks at the car.

I nod. —A wife murderer.

—Oh my, he says, running his hand over the hood. —He killed her in the car?

He looks disappointed when I say no, so I tell him that he did use the car to transport the body to the dump. He brightens again.

—Well, he says. —A wife murderer. He opens the door and slides in. He pats the seat contentedly, looking around him as if he is about to take an amusement-park ride. I decide to tell him about Debbie after we have left.

The hallways of Jerome's building smell of sweat and urine; we walk by a young child sitting in front of a closed door. She picks at a sore on her cheek and stares at us as we pass. Jerome's apartment, like mine, is a single room, though larger; there is a bathroom, and one wall is given over to what the ad probably called a kitchenette, though it is really just a sink and a small refrigerator stuck to the wall. The room is cluttered, but a clear effort has been made to divide it up into more or less traditional living areas—a bed and night table are in one corner, a small table sits in the kitchen area, and in the corner opposite the bed is a ratty couch and coffee table. Jerome puts his hands on his hips and looks around the room.

—What a dump, he says theatrically.

—It's not so bad, I say.

He looks at me and rolls his eyes, then gestures at the couch.
—Have a seat in the parlor, he says grandly. He walks to the middle of the room and stands, looking around. I stay by the door.
—I don't have a lot of time, I say, and he looks back at me impatiently, as if I were just another piece of baggage he has to pack.
—Girl, he says, —you can't rush a movie star.

The couch is nubby, and grimy to the touch; most of the underwires have sprung, and I sit on the edge while Jerome opens the door to his closet.

A mirror hangs from the back of the closet door, and as it swings around it gives me a quick jittering view of myself waiting here on the couch for him. The closet is stuffed full of clothes and Jerome kneels on the floor in front of it; he sighs, then leans in, emerging after a moment with an old brown suitcase, which he lays on the floor next to him; then he dives back in, this time coming out with a little square cosmetics case. He looks at the suitcases and shakes his head.

—These isn't enough, he says. —I can't fit it all in these.
—They have clothes in Hollywood, I say. —You can get a whole new wardrobe.

He sighs and stares into the closet, gazing at all the beautiful things he will have to leave behind, all the beautiful dresses and shoes and slips and scarves. By now, the show at the theater will have ended; Danny will come out of the darkness into the lobby, and go to his corner, where he will stand and fill his mouth with popcorn. As he chews, he will gaze at my bubble; he will wonder where I have gone.

—Listen, I say to Jerome, —you can send for your things. When you get out there, you can send for your things.

He pauses a moment, his hands buried in a colorful pile of scarves on the floor in front of him, and looks up, past me.

—Yes, he says dreamily, —I'll send for my things. He nods, gazing off: he will send for his things. It does not seem to occur to him to wonder whom exactly he will send for his things, or who will care for them when he is gone. In the world he is about to enter there are people for that, and for Jerome there will be an army of beautiful boys to retrieve his things and drive him places, and comb his hair, and care for him. But for now, he must decide. He stands and pulls out a dress; then swings the mirror around and holds the dress up in front of him. The dress is a yellow silky thing, printed with bright-green palm trees, and in the mirror, even without makeup, he is a beautiful woman, but from the back, in his black slacks and dowdy brown 7-Eleven smock, he just looks undernourished, like any skinny man you might walk behind in the street. He fans the skirt of the dress out, and turns his head slightly, look-ing coyly into the mirror. By now, Danny has turned to look for me in my bubble; by now, Debbie's owner has returned to his room to find her gone. Her water dish is full, on the floor in front of him. Debbie, he is saying, Debbie. He stares at the floor where he last saw her and wonders how she could have left him. He will spend his life finding her now. Debbie, he will call down side streets and alleys, Debbie. She was the only thing he loved.

—That's nice, I say to Jerome, —Take that one. He looks at me in the mirror, then carefully folds the dress up and lays it gently in the suitcase.

When he is finished, the suitcase is so full he needs my help to close it; I lean on it while Jerome snaps the clasps. Our faces are inches apart; I can see the tiny veins spidering out from an ugly bluish bruise on the side of his jaw. He looks at me sharply, then covers the bruise with his hand.

—What are you looking at? he says.

—Nothing, I say. —You have beautiful skin tone.

—Really? he says. He looks at me a moment, then turns to the mirror. Skin tone was something my sister was concerned with; she used to steal money from my mother's purse and from my father's dresser, and spend it on little tubes and jars of stuff that she spread across her face before going to bed at night. She would have beautiful skin, she told me, and I, I would be a dried-up old frog by the time I was thirty. She kept it all in a plastic bag, which she hid around our room; she used to accuse me of stealing it when she was not there, though right up until the day she left I can hardly remember a moment I spent in that room when she was not there.

Jerome caresses his face softly; his skin is streaked and mottled like marble, with fresh and fading bruises. He meets my eyes in the mirror.

—Skin tone is very important in Hollywood, he says. —All the big movie stars have it.

I stand. —Ready? I say, and he looks up at me in horror.

—Honey, he says. —Look at me.

He stands and plucks at the 7-Eleven smock, then suddenly unzips it and throws it to the floor, staring down at it a moment.

—Okay, I say, reaching for his suitcase, but he shakes his head and turns to enter the bathroom.

—You can't hurry beautiful, he says. He closes the door behind him.

A stack of fashion magazines sits on the table in front of the couch. The models on the covers cannot be the same as the models on the covers of my sister's magazines, but they look the same. They have the same faces and hair and figures. Next to the magazines is a small television; little balls of aluminum foil are wrapped around each of its antennae, but even so, it only gets a couple of channels, and both are fuzzy. A game show is playing on the clearest channel, and I leave it there, with the sound down. My father watched game shows. He watched everything, really, and he watched it all in the same way, with a slightly unfocused gaze and a drink on his knee. He watched news and game shows and dramas and comedies, even cartoons; there was always something going on in front of him. My mother paid no attention to the television except when there was a game show on, and those she watched with rapt attention, leaning forward in her chair. She didn't bother with the game itself, the questions and answers, but the prizes captivated her, particularly the extravagant ones—sailboats and cars, trips to Europe and Hawaii, whole housefuls of new furniture—she watched as they were won or lost, her mouth slightly open, forgetting even the ash on her cigarette, which would grow and fall to the floor. At the break, she turned to my father with an incriminating look; he kept his eyes on the television, watching the commercials as though they were part of the entertainment.

I sat behind them at a table doing my homework while they watched, answering the questions in my head; when I was correct, I wrote down what I would have won. I kept lists of all my prizes; I wrote them down in the margins of my homework, and I would get my assignments back with question marks next to things like "sailboat" and "bedroom suite." After a while, I began to keep lists of the prizes I did not win, and at some point I began to keep lists of things I wanted for myself: a husband, pets, a baby.

Once as I lay on my bed writing up a list, my sister slunk over and snatched it from my hand, then stood over me reading it. A sailboat? she said. What would I do with a sailboat? She looked at me, then took the list to her bed, and lay down to read it all the way through. When she finished, she looked at me. She would take all of those things from me, she said. They would all be hers: my sailboat and my dining-room suite and my swimming pool. And then she would steal my husband, she told me; she would change the names of my children and raise them as her own. They would forget my name. And my pets—she thought a moment about my pets—my pets she would poison, she finally said. She dropped the list on the floor and stared at the ceiling. Her hair fell away from her face, and as the muscle in her jaw worked, the scars along the side of her face jumped like a tangle of snakes moving just under the skin.

On Jerome's television, a woman stares, disappointed at a car she has apparently not won, and I turn it off. My sister did not usually join us watching television at night; after a point, she never joined us when we were together, but every now and then I heard the door to our room open, and then I could see her feet as she sat in shadows at the top of the stairs, watching television with the rest of us, though none of us were really watching it. There was a fragile togetherness then, something almost like a family, even if it was only for a moment, even if it was only that we were all occupied in wanting something at the same time, even if what we wanted was not the same thing.

Across from Jerome's building is another apartment house; most of its windows are shaded, but one is open, and a man stands near it in front of a mirror. He is dressed only in boxer shorts, and on a little table next to him is a heap of what look like the skins of small furry animals. The man is balding; he paws around in the heap, then picks one up and sets it on his head. It still looks like the skin of a small furry animal, though it is just a toupee. The man turns his head from side to side, looking at himself, then steps back a bit from the mirror and strikes a sort of tough-guy pose, narrowing his eyes, scowling at the mirror; suddenly he grins, then smiles, then laughs and nods. He tries out a few more expressions, then removes the toupee and tries another, going through more or less the same series of poses.

I watch him try several; they all look about the same, like little pets perched on top of his head. Finally, he seems to settle on one; he picks up a hand mirror and turns his back to the larger mirror, to see himself from the rear. Our eyes meet as he turns; he is not much more than twenty yards away from me, so close I can see the mismatch in the color of his hair and the color of the toupee. I smile, and he stares back at me a moment, then abruptly reaches out and pulls down the window shade, giving me an ugly look just before he disappears. From the bathroom, I hear a little shriek, then silence, and I stand just outside listening before I knock.

—I have to get going, I say, and the door opens suddenly; Jerome's face is made up now, the bruises caked over with powder, his eyelids smeared bright blue behind thick black false eyelashes. His hair is in a cloud around his head.

—I can't go, he says, with a kind of snippy hysteria. —Look at me. I'm too fat. He brushes past me and stands at the mirror; his blue dress is unzipped to the waist, and under his slip, the knobs of his spine poke through. He shakes his head.

—I'm a cow, he says. —A big huge cow.

—No, I say. —You look beautiful. Like a model. His eyes meet mine in the mirror, and they narrow, gauging my sincerity.

—Really? he says softly. —A model? I nod, and he looks back at himself, running his eyes unhappily up and down the length of his body. He bunches the loose material of the dress at his waist.

—Look at me, he says. —I've let myself go.

—Listen, I say. —I'll take your suitcase out now, okay? He nods, not looking at me.

—They're going to love you, I tell him, and he stares at himself a moment, then nods.

—That's right, he says. —They're going to love me. He leans close to the mirror. —You're going to be a big star, he says. —They're going to love you. They're all going to love you. He gazes deeply into his own eyes, then closes them slowly, and brings his lips to the glass in a soft lingering kiss.

I lay Jerome's suitcase on the back seat, and reach down onto the floor to feel for Debbie; she is there, a soft beating thing under my hand.

—Debbie, I say, —we're going to Hollywood. There is no response, just the dry shift of bones under her fur as she moves.

Live girls

On my way back to Jerome's apartment, I begin a list in my head of the things I will buy for Debbie when we reach a final destination: a little soft bed with a fluffy pink pillow; a tiny sweater for the cold evenings; perhaps even a little wooden house of her own. It is something Danny could make for her– the house, maybe the bed. I do not think Danny would like living with Debbie. I do not think he is thinking of me now. He is sitting in his seat in the theater; outside, men are lining up, but he is not thinking of them. He is gazing up at the women on the screen; he is wondering what it would be like if they were live, and he is wondering what it would be like to touch them; he is wondering what their skin feels like, if it is as smooth as wood, as soft and as smooth as the things he carves of wood.

Jerome does not answer my knock, and when, after a moment, I push open the door, he is perched on the edge of the couch, talking on the phone. He acknowledges my presence with an annoyed look, and makes a show of turning his back to me.

—That's right, baby, he says. —Hollywood. Next time you see me, it'll cost you seven-fifty. He is quiet a moment, then says, —That's where you're wrong. I'm not going to miss you one bit. Besides, I got me a new man. A movie director. He pauses, then adds, —I'm going to send for my things.

He is silent for a long time, and I wonder if Eric may have hung up on him, but when I say his name, he shushes me, so I sit on the edge of his bed to wait. On the wall there, he has tacked up two Polaroids, one of Eric and one of himself. They seem to be at the same party; each picture has similar background details and faces. Half of Eric's picture has been cut away, though you can still see the shoulder of a woman who was standing next to him, and a strand or two of her hair. The two pictures have been jammed together so that Eric and Jerome appear to be standing side by side, looking at each other. The way the light has caught him, the bruises on Jerome's cheek shimmer like jewels just under the surface of the skin.

—Uh-huh, Jerome says behind me, —well, don't you count on it. Then he hangs the phone up with a bang. I stand, not looking at him.

—Well, I say heartily, —let's go.

He is still on the couch, gazing out the window, his hands in his lap; when he turns to look at me, his eyes are trembling with tears. I walk to the door, and after a moment he rises and picks up his little cosmetics case, but as he follows me to the door, he stops and stands in the middle of the room, looking slowly around. Everything here is cheap and worn; there is nothing anyone would want, but he gazes around as if he is looking upon a roomful of treasures. He picks up a little blue plastic vase. The vase holds a dusty paper flower, and Jerome holds it to his nose and closes his eyes, breathing in, as though the flower has a scent.

—You can send for it, I say, and he looks at me, then nods and puts the vase down. As we leave, he closes the door softly, with barely a click, as if he does not want to alert his things that he is leaving them.

The little girl is back in the hallway, at the top of the stairs, her back to us; she is hunched like a cat, staring down at something on the step in front of her. Jerome brushes past her with an irritated little tsk, but I look down to see what she is watching. It is just a bug, a beetle or water bug, struggling to free itself from a clump of dust in the corner of the step.

Once he is in his seat, Jerome begins immediately to fiddle with things, rolling the window up and down, pushing buttons on the radio, though the car engine isn't yet on. He pulls down the front visor and gasps with delight when he sees it is equipped with a little mirror, then again when he realizes the mirror has a tiny light; he switches it on and off a few times, admiring himself both ways, then flips the visor up and sits back, pleased. He has his own mirror with its own light; he is riding in the car of a man who killed his wife; he is going to be a movie star.

—Girl, let's go, he says, as if I have kept him waiting for hours.

—I ain't getting any younger.

It's a dark night, and I'm not sure where I am or where I'm heading, but I pull away from the curb.

—Ooh, Jerome says. —Ooh, ooh. Slow down.

He rolls down his window as we approach a little cluster of hookers on the corner.

—Yoo-hoo, girls, he calls out, and they look up at us.

—Slow down, he says, swatting at me. He pushes his shoulders out the window, and I slow to a stop.

—Oh, girls, he sings out to the women. —I'm going to *Hollywood*. I'm going to be a *movie* star.

The women stare at him a moment; a bitter, chill wind has come up, and their faces are tight in the cold. They're all wearing miniskirts or hot pants; they stand close together, their hands cupped around cigarettes, and they look at Jerome as if he is a creature from another world, speaking words they have never heard. Finally, one shakes her head. —Hollywood, she says with a derisive little snort; she rolls her eyes and turns away. The others do the same, except for one, who takes a step toward the car. She is younger than the others, perhaps a teenager, though it's hard to tell her age from the makeup and the cold. Her face is angry and she stares past Jerome at me; just as I pull away, she holds her arm out and flicks her cigarette at us, but it misses the window and bounces off the door. Jerome pulls himself back into the car.

—See you in the movies, he calls out, then bounces back against the seat.

—Humph, he says. —They just jealous. He begins to arrange himself, fluffing out his hair, smoothing his dress out along his legs, like a cat cleaning itself after falling from a chair. I drive through the dark streets, which are more or less quiet now; there are a few junkies, some hookers, but mostly stray men, drifting alone like ghosts in the air, without feet or faces.

Debbie is silent in back, and Jerome watches the streets as I drive. I am lost within minutes, and though I drive with as much confidence as I can fake, before long the road I have taken dead-ends right at the water's edge. A streetlamp lights up the dirty beach, catching the glint of bottles and cans; scraps of paper skitter across the sand.

The submarine base is visible from here, just across the water, sending up black plumes of soot into the gray sky. Jerome looks at me.

—That ain't Hollywood, honey, he says gently. I nod.

—I know, I say. We both stare out at the water.

—I lost my map, I say. —I had the route all figured out.

Jerome looks down at the seat around him, then leans forward and pops open the glove compartment, peers inside, then pulls out a pair of gloves, which he lays on his lap; it occurs to me that Danny may be one of the few people who actually keep gloves in their glove compartments. Next, Jerome takes out a movie brochure; from the cover a woman gazes out, eyes lidded, tongue between her teeth, hands not quite covering her bare breasts. *Hundreds of Titles,* the brochure promises, *Hotter Than Hot.* Across the bottom, in yellow letters, is printed *Live Girls–Live Action.* Jerome stares down at it, then looks up at me, raising an eyebrow.

—That's not mine, I say. —It belongs to a friend.

—Mm-hmm, he says, then puts the brochure on top of the gloves. Next he pulls out a map, then another, then two or three more, laying them one after another on the seat.

—Girl, he says. —You got maps for every place. He pushes them all at me, then goes back to rooting around in the glove compartment. There is a map for every region of the country, and one of the country as a whole; with these maps Danny could have gone anywhere, though he told me once that he had never been out of the state. Hollywood is a tiny dot outside of Los Angeles, a drive of days, perhaps a week, and Phoenix, though it is closer, is not closer by much. Next to me, Jerome flips through the brochure.

—*Honey*, he murmurs at a picture of a woman with her shirt open, —button up.

To get to either Hollywood or Phoenix, we would have to drive for days through cold states full of snow and wind and long empty stretches of land. Directly south on the map, much closer, is Florida, a drive of maybe three or four days, one that would let us hug the coast all the way.

I have been there once. As children, my sister and I were taken there to meet our grandparents, though we had never met them before, or heard anything from or about them. On the drive down, my sister told me that the reason we were going was that my grandparents were going to choose one of us to keep for their own; the other one would have to go back to Ohio with my parents. I did not believe her at first, but driving down, staring at the backs of my parents' heads, and their tense, knotty necks, it began to seem plausible that they might prefer to have only one of us. The rest of the way, I drifted in and out of sleep; in my dreams, my grandparents were kindly, white-haired people, Santa Claus-like in their concern and interest. They would love us both; they would keep us both. They would be too kind to take only one of us.

We arrived at night, to a tiny dark house; my sister and I were put to bed on a couch, one of us at either end. When I tried to lie down, my sister pulled her legs up suddenly, as if to touch my skin would burn her own, then sat huddled up at her end; I did the same, and we hunched there all night, like two animals forced to share the same cage. Outside the window nearest us, my grandparents had installed a fluorescent bug-killer. Every few seconds, it crackled with the electric hiss of an insect burning out, and in the quick purple flare I could see my sister's face, her eyes flashing with the sizzle of the light.

—They liked me best, she whispered, though we had spent only five or ten minutes with them so far. —They're going to keep me.

She would have her own room, she said, with a tankful of tropical fish in the corner, and a collection of seashells on her dresser. She would go to the beach every day to collect them; she would live in the sun.

When I went to the bathroom, I could hear my grandparents talking in their room. —Such a pretty little girl, I heard my grandmother say. —The one.

All night I dreamed of the two of us, crouched at the water's edge, sifting through the sand for our seashells.

In the few days that followed, my grandparents showed no signs of deliberating between us; they showed almost no interest in us at all, in fact, or in my father, whose parents they were but to whom they seemed to have as little connection as he to us. He spent most of the trip sitting in a chair alone on the patio, gazing at the lawn. Every now and then, my mother would look out at him and shake her head, sighing pointedly, but my grandparents ignored her too. Aside from listening to twice-hourly weather reports on the radio, their primary concern seemed to be the extermination of every insect that had the misfortune to wander into or near their house. There was the bug-killer outside, which stayed on even during the day, and besides that there was poison everywhere—little ant traps in the middle of each room; lines of boric acid running along every wall, fly strips hanging just outside every window. It was like a festival of insect death—flies and bees struggling to free themselves from the sticky fly strips, half-dead beetles and ants dragging themselves along the floor—but even so, the house was still full of bugs, and my grandparents were always watching for them, always jerking around at any sudden flicking movement in the room, and then my grandfather would go flapping after it with a grimy worn flyswatter that was always close at hand. Their windows were splotchy with the corpses of squashed bugs. My grandfather seemed never to be still—even during a meal, he would suddenly lurch from the table, flatten a bug against a wall or window, then come back to his meal and resume eating, the flyswatter in his lap as though he had not even left.

We fit into their routine as best we could, and for the most part they seemed not to notice us, except that every now and then a strange dark lull would fall over things, and I would look up to see my grandparents staring at my sister's face; they would gaze at her for long blank moments, until she became aware of them and either turned her face away or stared back, and then they would look not too quickly away.

Whenever we went outdoors, even to the backyard, my grandmother insisted on keeping my sister's face covered with a large sun hat and big black sunglasses. That sun will burn the skin right off her face, she'd say to my mother, though the same precautions were not taken for me. It was a confused, exhausting trip, spent mostly in silence; we were not far from the ocean, and I could smell it in the air, but we were never taken to it.

Finally, on our last day, something provoked someone to drive us to a sea park. It was a run-down place, without much business; many of the holding tanks were empty, and what fish there were swam listlessly back and forth behind the dusty glass walls of their tanks. One room was occupied by a single tank set up in the middle of the floor. A giant squid was heaped forlornly in the corner, its long arms in a messy tangle. Its head was slumped onto the floor, and it hardly bothered to follow us with its eyes as we circled its tank.

Outside, there was a little pool with some fish in it, for people to swim in, and somehow I found myself sitting in the corner, underwater, wearing a little mask and snorkel. The water was murky and my mask fogged up immediately, so all I could make out were the blurry shapes of fish hovering at the opposite wall of the pool. I sat where I was, waiting for something to happen, and just as I was about to leave the pool, a skate glided toward me, a huge flat thing the size of a garbage-can lid, its enormous black wings flapping at its sides. At the last moment, I saw its tiny black eyes fixed on me and I put up my arms, whether to catch it or keep it away, I don't remember now, but for a moment, before it veered away, I touched it, and for that moment the skate seemed almost to rest there between my arms; I could feel its muscles tense, then release, and under the skin, the beat of something against my arms. I did not want to let it go.

My sister watched jealously from the side of the pool; she had refused to change into a bathing suit and so was not allowed into the water, and there she sat, hidden under my grandmother's huge sunglasses and the wide sun hat, though the day was overcast. I could see her from where I was in the pool, a blur through my mask and the water.

—That thing was ugly, she told me when I got out of the pool. She said it was all scarred, from where they caught it with the hooks. I looked back, and could just see it through the cloudy water, a black triangle, moving fluidly around the pool.

That night was our last, and she huddled at her end of the couch and stared at me.

—They're deciding right now, she said, and as I sat there watching insects sputter against the bug light, I wasn't sure which would be the best thing–to be left here with those people or to return home alone with my parents. They would choose her, my sister said, but in the morning she had her suitcase packed and sitting by the door before I even woke up.

She was more sullen than usual as we drove back to Ohio, and she refused to leave the car, even to use the bathroom, until it was dark out. And all the way home, I kept thinking it was still possible: it was possible that we would go back; it was possible that they would want us both; it was possible that we would be taken out of our dark room and allowed to live our lives together under the bright sun, sitting by the sea and watching the bright water come up to meet our feet. And then we arrived at our house, and got out of the car and walked up the stairs to our beds.

Next to me, Jerome has turned on the little light attached to his visor; he is modeling Danny's gloves, holding his hands up to his face in various poses. In the dim glow, his bruises are hardly visible, and the swelling of his lips gives him a kind of blurry glamour. He sighs, then switches off the light and sits back, still wearing Danny's gloves. He looks at me, and I wonder what I am going to do with him. I smile and make a U-turn. As we head toward the highway, he leans back and closes his eyes.
—Wake me when we get there, he says.
In the rearview mirror, the moon shines over the Sound. Like a huge black animal, a submarine breaks the surface of the sea, then just as suddenly submerges again. My last sight of the water is a dark, still, shining plain, its surface unruffled by the huge things lumbering about beneath it.

By the time we reach the highway, Dave is starting the last show; we will be in another state before it ends. Danny will stand guard over his popcorn and then, when there is no one to see him, he will slip into the theater. He will close his eyes in the darkness and think of me and wonder where I have gone; when I come back, he tells himself, he will never let me go, and when the evening ends and I have not returned, he will stand at the glass doors and stare out at the street, wondering how I could have left him. Behind him, Dave will stand at the door of his office and watch him, lighting cigarettes, then dropping them, leaving them to smolder, forgotten, on the floor.
Soon Danny will move to my bubble, where he will look at the picture I have left of the woman in the cave, and think she is my

sister. How pretty she is, he will think, how soft and smooth her skin, her hair, her neck. If only he could touch her, if only she were live? Before long, he will forget me and dream of her, and when he closes his eyes in the theater, it is her face he will remember. Soon he will forget my face, and think of me only occasionally; perhaps, at work, watching a pigeon beat its wings against the wire he has put up to trap it, he will stare into its flat little pigeon eyes and wish there were something he could do to help it. Then he will turn away.

Beside me, Jerome is silent, his eyes closed. His face is like a mask, brightening and fading in the lights of passing trucks, as still and perfect as the face of a corpse. Behind me, Debbie is silent as well.

—Debbie, I whisper, and wait, but there is not a sound. They are sleeping things I carry with me as I leave the city.

Behind us, the movie plays on, and Dave slumps in his chair, lost in a dream of heat and sun and sand. He is in Arizona, and at his side is his wife. He killed her so many years ago, but here she is beside him. He has not killed her after all. She smiles at him, and he turns to her. His cigarette falls from his hand, dropping into a heap of brochures, which begins slowly to smolder, but he is dreaming; his wife opens her arms to him and he enters them. They will be together forever. All around him brochures are igniting. Hot action, they say, as page after page goes up in fire, bodies bursting into flames. A quiet line of fire creeps from his office out into the lobby, and in the theater the men feel their skin grow hot; their blood warms with the heat, and Danny stands, looking down at his hands. They are on fire; fire races up his arms, and he watches himself burn. Outside, the glass doors melt and fire spreads through the city. On the hill, the girls look down and shake their heads at the conflagration below them: sinners are burning. They smile: God will protect them, they say, and they turn their backs on the burning city. They do not see the ribbons of fire snaking up the hill, and they go calmly to bed, safely held in the dreams of God. When they wake, their beds are in flames. Jesus, they whisper, save us. Jesus, they call, running up and down their halls, girls alive with fire.

And in the theater, Danny burns, thinking of all that we would have had together. All of it is lost: our little house turns to ash, all the wooden birds fall burning from the trees, and our children erupt in flames. Mother, they call, Mother, we are burning, and in her room my sister beats her wings against the walls. *Save me,* she whispers as the heat melts the skin from her face. *Save me.* Spiders of fire scuttle across my heart.

I drive all night. Morning comes as a gloomy red fog to my left. I had thought that driving for so long would take us someplace different, and I expected the sun to rise over a sunny, warm, beautiful place, but we seem not to have gotten far: it's chilly, rainy, gray. Inside the car there is no sound at all; in back, Debbie is as still as a stone. When we arrive at our destination, I will find a little patch of sunny grass to put her in; she will have a yard of her own, and we will have a little house, where we will live happily, the three of us. Danny, Dave, Eric—all the people we have left behind will be nothing but ashes in a city of ashes, and we will live in the sun. The bruises will fade from Jerome's face. We will wear each other's clothes, and in the evenings we will sit on our porch and watch the ocean roll in the distance. One day we will marry and live in little houses next to each other; our husbands will be friends, and on the weekends we will take our children to the sea park. We will have the lives we were meant to have, all of us, and when Debbie sleeps on my feet at night, illness and death will be nothing more than the dream of a dozing animal.

—Debbie, I whisper, —we're going to Florida. We're going to live by the sea. Next to me, Jerome stirs and murmurs under his ratty fur coat, then rolls his sleeping face toward me. Mascara has smeared in dark puddles under his eyes, and in the cold morning light his bruises are like ugly blue and purple fruit under his pale-brown skin. His eyelashes tremble, but he does not wake, even as I pull into a service area for gas.

As the tank fills, I reach for Debbie on the floor behind my seat; she lets out a faint mew of protest, but allows me to pull her out and set her gently on the back seat, where she looks around, then lays her head on her paws. Jerome is awake by the time the tank is full; he lifts his head and turns it foggily from side to side. I replace the gas nozzle, and when I turn, he is gazing at me. I smile, but he looks at me as if he has never seen me before. As I leave to go into the service station, he lowers his visor, and snaps on the little mirror light.

Inside, two women lean on the counter, sharing a cigarette. They nod at me, then go back to their conversation. At the end of the counter is a little station with coffee and a tray of doughnuts; as I fill two cups of coffee, Jerome enters, his fur draped like a robe over his shoulders, carrying his cosmetics case. His hair is straggly and tangled, his face still puffy from sleep, but even so, he strolls through the store like royalty.

—Excuse me, he says as he sweeps past me. —There's a *animal* in that car.

The women at the counter watch him, and when he goes into the women's room, they exchange a look, then glance at me.

—Do you have any milk? I ask. —For my cat. One nods at a little pitcher and I pour some into a cup, then put two doughnuts into a bag.

Debbie opens her eyes when I kneel on the seat next to her; she looks at the little cup of cream, then at me.

She sniffs at the cream, then looks at me again and puts her head back on her paws. When I look up, Jerome is standing several feet from the car, watching us. I pour the rest of Debbie's cream into my cup and stand.

—Ready? I say, but he gives me a baleful glance, then looks back at Debbie.

—You could have told me there was a animal, he says.

—It's just a cat, I tell him. He edges closer to the car and peers in through the window as if Debbie is a bomb that might go off with a glance. She is cleaning her paws, and he watches her a moment, then straightens, his arms folded across his chest.

—I can't be riding with no cat, he says. He looks around the parking lot as if he is deciding on another car to travel in.

—You have to, I say. —It belongs to my sister. I promised I'd bring her. He looks back at me.

—And besides, I add, —she's just a little cat. You wouldn't have known she was there if I hadn't put her on the seat.

—Excuse me, he says. —I would have known. I could smell it. I smelled it the minute I got in the car.

—You didn't say anything, I say. He sniffs haughtily.

—My mama didn't raise me to be talking about how people's cars smell.

I lean into the back seat and bring my face close to Debbie; she smells like a cold empty room, with a faint scent of flowers, as though someone wearing Jerome's perfume has walked in for just a moment, then left.

—She doesn't smell, I tell him, and he sniffs again, looking around.

—Well, he says, —some people is just not as sensitive as others. It's a gift, he adds.

—Uh-huh, I say. —Well, we have to take her. Anyways, she's sick; she won't bother you.

He rolls his eyes. —Oh, he says, —that's just fine. A sick cat. That'll turn people's heads.

I get in and start the car; Jerome approaches it reluctantly, then opens his door, sets his case on the floor, and sits gingerly on his seat as if the whole car has been contaminated. He breathes in deeply, then shudders.

—Cat, he says, as if he were saying "garbage" or "dirt." I take a doughnut from the bag and offer it to him. He stares at it, then at the bag in my lap and finally looks at me.

—Don't you tempt me, he says. He turns his face away and he is silent as I pull out of the parking lot; he is silent as I drive, silent as I eat my doughnut. Even over the noise of the car and the rush of the tires on the road, I can hear myself chew and swallow; I can feel the food pushing down my throat, and I can feel Jerome's eyes on my mouth, my neck, but when I turn to look at him, he is staring at the landscape out his window, a dull panorama of industrial parks.

—This is ugly, he says. He sighs. —I want to see something beautiful. He lowers his visor and gazes at himself in the mirror. A heavy coat of makeup more or less covers the bruises on his face, though his eye is still swollen. A speck of blood gleams on his neck from a shaving cut; he presses the tip of his finger against it a moment, then touches the finger to his tongue.

I put the doughnut back in the bag, and drive as if I know where we are going, as if I have some place to take us, but as the sun bleaches the sky white, I feel as if we are disappearing into it. The highway is packed with cars full of families and Christmas presents. The faces of children appear at windows, gazing at us as we pass. I head south, but every mile feels like nothing at all, as if what we are leaving behind is riding with us, pulling us back as we try to pull away. Soon Jerome will wonder where I am taking him. He sighs loudly, then again, until I look at him.

—Did I say this was ugly? he asks, then sighs again and snaps on the radio; he turns the dial from static to static, finally settling on the clearest signal, then sits back with another loud unhappy sigh.

I can feel him again, watching me, but when I turn to look at him, he is staring out the window at a little girl in the car next to us; her face is at the window and she is gazing at Jerome. After a moment, he sticks his tongue out at her, but she just continues to stare at him. The driver of the car turns to look at us, and I speed up.

—Monster, Jerome says. —Little kids is nothing but monsters. They should be seen and not heard. He looks back at the little girl. —They shouldn't even be seen.

I pull into the lane in front of the car; in the rearview mirror, the father is just driving, and next to him a woman's head is bent—over a book, perhaps. A child sleeps in the back, next to the girl who was watching Jerome. They are all being driven somewhere; they know where they are headed, and sooner or later they will get there. I wish for a moment I were in the back seat with those children, a child in a car that someone else is driving.

—We used to take trips all the time, I tell Jerome, —when I was growing up.

He sighs, not looking at me. —You said you was a orphan, he says.

—We were adopted, I tell him. —My sister and me.

He looks at me. —You was adopted? he says, and I nod.

—We lived in Florida, I say. —We used to go on trips a lot. We went to the sea park every weekend.

—Sea park? he asks. He holds his hands out in front of him, and examines his nails.

—It's this place, I tell him, —where they have fish. Whales. Skates. Squids.

—Whales, he says. —I'm a whale. He looks down at his lap. —A big fat whale.

He pokes a finger into his leg; it goes nowhere. —Look at that, he says. —Nothing but blubber. He slaps his leg. —Slow down, he says to me. —I can't get there looking like this.

I slow down and he settles back, putting his coat across his lap while the car with the little girl passes us; as it pulls away, I can see little round heads bobbing at the back window like identical white moons. The radio goes completely to static, and Jerome's long arm appears from under his coat to change the station. He twists the knob until he comes to music, then turns up the volume and leans back again, with a loud sigh, closing his eyes.

—We'll be there soon, I say, and he opens one eye, looks at me, then closes it again, like a suspicious bird.

He snaps his fingers softly to the music, and I drive; I feel as if I am driving us into a dark cold sea.

I drive all day. Watching Debbie in the rearview mirror, I can tell she is asleep by the occasional twitch of a paw or a whisker. Jerome has covered himself with his coat; he is all fur but for his head. His face is completely still but for the tiny throb of a muscle beating just at the corner of his eye. Whenever I think he has at last fallen asleep, his hand slides out to change the radio station. Sometimes his lips move with the song, and every now and then I hear the hum of a tune in his throat, but he keeps his eyes closed until I pull into a truck stop for gas.

He watches me fill the tank and when I head in to pay, he gets out of the car and follows me inside, where there is a little coffee shop. It's divided in half—truckers on one side, in a separated area marked off by a sign, and on the other side everyone else, mostly families. We take a booth in the family room. Most of the truckers are at the counter in their area, jammed together elbow to elbow. They eat quickly, stopping only to smoke or take a sip of coffee, and every now and then they look over at us.

When Jerome orders only water, the waitress looks at him over her pad. —*Water?* she says, and he nods without looking at her. He is gazing at the truckers.

—Oooh, he says, —let's sit over there.

—We can't, I say. —It's just for truckers. He looks at me, then back at the men.

When my food comes, Jerome stares at it and watches it go into my mouth until I push the plate away, toward him.

—Get that away from me, he says. —You devil. He takes a sip of his water and looks at the truckers.

—I've heard them truckers is *wild*, he says. He watches them a while, then stands.

—Honey, he says, —you finish up here. I'm going to powder my nose.

He crosses the room to the truckers' side, then walks along the low wall to the bathroom, with an exaggerated female glide. Several of the truckers watch him, only their eyes moving as they sit hunched over coffee and cigarettes. I lay money on the table and head out, past the bathrooms, into a little store; it's full of things for travelers: clothing, hardware, even toys; at the back are two full racks of magazines. I stop to look them over; they are all sex magazines. A man stands at the rack next to me, slowly flipping through one, gazing down at each picture a moment before he turns the page. He glances up at me, but doesn't close the magazine; I can feel his eyes on me as I buy a little carton of milk for Debbie.

The men's and women's bathrooms are side by side. The women's room is empty, and I push open the door of the men's room and call Jerome's name. A line of men stands at the urinals. —Hey, honey, come on in here, one of them says as they all turn to look at me, and I close the door.

Debbie drinks a bit of milk from her little cup. With my finger I stroke the smooth top of her head; her ears flatten and she stops drinking until I move my hand. I lean back on the side of the car. It is late afternoon sliding into evening; it is chilly still, but the sun is growing warm as we move south. I close my eyes; the sun is a warm hand over my face. I drift under it, and what I see is home, though it is a home I have never seen before. My sister waves at me from an upstairs window; her face is a round

pale moon. Black wings beat the air behind her. *Come home,*
she says.

When I open my eyes, Jerome is standing a few feet away, looking at me.

I feel dazed and wonder how long I have been dozing, how long
he has been watching me.

—Girl, he says. —Where was you?

—I looked everywhere for you, I say, and he smiles. His lips are
swollen, bluish.

—I was making friends, he says.

—I looked everywhere, I repeat. My head buzzes from sleep. In
the back seat, Debbie's head is on her paws. I can't tell how
much of her milk she drank, and I empty out the little cup and
close up the container. Jerome turns to look back at the truck
stop as we pull away; rows of trucks are lined up next to it, like
animals waiting to be fed.

Jerome is asleep in minutes; his whole head is hidden under his
coat. In the back seat, Debbie is still; now and then she lets out
a little sigh. The rush of the road underneath us is a soothing
hum. Everything is behind us, and for a moment, as darkness
falls, it seems almost as if we have reached our destination, as
if this—the night, the hum of the car, the occasional soft light
of a passing truck—were where we were headed. I would like to
stop time now, in this moment, before it all disappears.

Come to me, my sister says from her window. Her face is a
round circle without features, and behind her the air throbs;
her black wings throb. *Come to me,* she says, *come home to me.*

I startle at the long bleat of a horn, coming from a truck only a
foot or so away. I edge the car back into my own lane; there is a
throb in my throat, a beating behind my eyes. Neither Jerome
nor Debbie has awakened, and I drive the car straight ahead,

but soon I can feel myself drifting again, and when I come to a little rest area with several motels, I pull off. All the parking lots are packed with cars, so I choose what looks like the cheapest. I've parked and left the car before Jerome wakes; as I enter the office, I see his head emerge from under his coat, like a turtle poking out of its shell.

The woman inside the office is watching a tiny television on the counter; when I ask for two rooms, she glances away from the television only briefly to scan a list, then looks back at the screen.

—We've just got the one left, she says; she pushes a form and a key toward me. I take the key and fill out the form. Everything I write is a lie except for the name; I put down my sister's name, then sign under it. I can feel the woman watching me, but when I look up, it is only her face that's turned toward me; her eyes are still on the television. She is watching cartoons.

When I get in the car, Jerome leans over toward me and lowers his voice. —That cat hasn't moved, he says. —I've been watching it the whole time. He glances quickly back at Debbie. —I think it's dead, he whispers, speaking slowly, enunciating each word.

I look in the rearview mirror; Debbie could be a stuffed animal left there by a child.

—She's tired, I say, —it's been a long drive.

—Humph, he says. —It's not natural to be that quiet.

He sits back and settles under his coat; he looks cozy and expectant, as though he is about to be taken somewhere. There are no parking places close to our room, so I give Jerome the key and let him out by the door, with his suitcases, then drive around to find a place.

Jerome is right about Debbie; even when I open her door, she doesn't move, and I feel uneasy to pick her up, afraid she'll already be stiff and cold, but her fur is warm and she opens her eyes when I slide my hands under her. She lets me hold her as I lock the car, and when a breeze ruffles the fur on top of her head, she lets me smooth it down. Against my chest I can feel the pump and wheeze of her tiny lungs.

It takes Jerome several minutes to answer my knock, and even then he doesn't open the door.
—Who's there? he says, on the other side of the door.
—Who do you think? I say. —Open the door.
He lets out a long exasperated huff. —I'm not decent, he says, —hold on, and in a few minutes he cracks the door open against a chain and peers out at us.
—Now what? he asks. The television is on behind him.
—It's cold, I say. —Let us in. He looks down at Debbie in my arms.
—No, ma'am, he says. —That cat is not coming in my room.
—Our room.
He looks at me. —There was just the one left, I say, and he looks past me out at the parking lot.
—Just one? he says. —In a big place like this?
He edges the door toward me, narrowing the opening between us.
—It's Christmas, I say. —Everyone is traveling.
He gazes at Debbie a long time, then looks out at the parking lot again. —Christmas? he says, and I nod.
—It's freezing out here, I say, though really it is quite mild, and he looks at Debbie again, then closes the door abruptly. I hear the chain rattle and fall, but then nothing happens, and I wait a moment, then try the door and open it.
Jerome is across the room, standing in front of a little open closet, arranging clothes; clothes are on the floor by his feet, and clothes are spread out all across one of the beds. The bed by the window is empty, and I walk past Jerome and lay Debbie on the pillow.
—I was planning on sleeping there, Jerome says, but when I turn, he is staring down at a stack of blouses on his bed, as if he has not said anything at all.

Next to the sink is a little stack of paper cups; I fill one with water and hold it by Debbie, who hunches over it and begins to drink. She drinks so much and for so long that even Jerome stops what he is doing to watch. When I take the cup to the sink to refill it, he moves quickly from the bed to stand in front of the closet. He spreads his arms.

—I'm going to need most of this closet, he says.

—We're only staying a night, I tell him. —You don't have to hang everything up.

—Well, he says, —I'm not going to be some old wrinkled thing. As Debbie drinks more water, he hangs up the rest of his things—several bright dresses, his fur coat, even a few slips; then he lines up three or four pairs of high heels neatly on the floor under the dresses. Even from across the room I can see how cheap it all is—dresses made of polyester to look like silk, huge high heels from some discount store. Even the fur is cheap and patchwork, like skins of several different kinds of animals collected from along the roadside. He turns and sees me watching him.

—Those are nice dresses, I say. He looks at me suspiciously.

—They're for Hollywood, he says. —Don't you get any ideas.

I sit on the edge of the bed and turn up the television; it is the usual local news, but with a Christmas theme—holiday weather, holiday traffic, holiday fatalities. The only thing out of the ordinary is a report of an accident between a tractor trailer and a circus truck headed south for the winter; several of the circus animals escaped. The manager of the circus is being interviewed at the scene.

—An elephant, the manager says, —a couple of the cats. Some monkeys. We're still checking.

Behind him, a brightly painted truck lies on its side and there are the noises of uneasy animals. Past the truck is a wide-open field, and beyond that, woods. The field is dusted with frost.

—Well, Jerome says, —time to change.

Live girls

The circus manager shakes his head. —These animals are tame, he says. —More or less. They can't really survive in the wild. They're used to cages.

—Excuse me? Jerome says, and I turn. He is standing by the door, which he has opened a few inches. —Can you give a girl a little privacy?

The sky is bright and full of stars, with a few drifting wisps of clouds; a hundred yards or so away is the highway, surprisingly busy for the time of night. They are all going somewhere, travelers with destinations. According to statistics, some percentage of them are doomed by the odds to end up holiday fatalities—no matter what they do, no matter what their plans are, or how they drive, or what they want. It is somehow their fate and it has nothing to do with them. Perhaps even the family we saw today, that little girl at the window watching Jerome—they may be already dead.

Most of the motel windows are dark. Behind them are sleeping families, any one of which could be mine, could have been mine. It's nothing more than a simple accident of birth. For a while my sister believed, or told me she believed, that there had been a terrible accident when she was born, that somehow she had been switched at the hospital with another baby. Her real parents would have loved her, and cared for her; they would not have let anything bad happen to her. Everything that had happened to her, all of it, had been meant to happen to someone else. There was another girl somewhere with my sister's life, with all the things she had been meant to have. She herself was not my sister, she said, and because she was not my sister, she did not have to love me.

In the dark rooms, children sleep; in the dark cars rushing by on the highway, children sleep. Somewhere in the fields and back roads, circus animals are loose—tigers and elephants wander along the highway, monkeys and bears creep through the suburbs. All night, animals will hunch beside fences, watching cows graze in the frosty fields; all night they will crouch at the side of the road, their eyes lit by passing headlights, their brains a confusion of images: jungle, circus, trees, cages. They are unable to tell what they remember from what they long for. Not knowing, they cannot move. Confused by their confused memories, there is no place for them to go. They are cold, and there is something they miss, but they do not know what it is.

When I knock at the door, the noise of the television goes down, then back up, and I knock again; Jerome appears after a while, his head wrapped in a towel, dressed in a silky kimono covered with a pattern of birds. He looks past me into the parking lot, as if someone else, someone better, might be following me in. He is damp, just washed, but he does not smell clean.

He goes to stand in front of the television, his back to me, and I pass behind him to get to my bed; I am not tired, but I get under the covers and roll onto my side away from him. After a little while, I hear the soft rustle of silk, and then I can feel him looming above me, blotting out the light, though my eyes are closed. He is silent but for the noise of his breath; then he leans closer. I can feel his breath on my face.

—Are you going to sleep like that? he finally says. —All dressed like that, with that cat?

I keep my eyes closed. —I left my pajamas in the car, I say, and he is quiet a moment.

—Uh-huh, he says, then rustles off. His bed shifts, then sighs, as he lies down; all the lights are still on and the television. I roll over to face him. He is on his back, wearing a little black eye mask.

—What about the lights? I say. He lifts up the corner of his mask and peeks out at me.

—I thought you was still up, he says. —All dressed and all.

I put my head on my pillow. I can feel Debbie at the bottom of the bed, solid against my feet. I close my eyes.

—I didn't plan on sleeping with no cat, Jerome says.

I nod. I am not tired, but when I open my eyes, the lights are out; only the television is still on, and in the shadowy light it casts, I can make out Jerome's face, the mask like a black bar over his eyes.

I have got used to sleeping alone in the years since my sister moved out. I was pleased when my roommate at the college found another room; it was hard to sleep with her there. There was the praying, and the stillness, and sometimes she ate candy bars at night, in the dark. I could hear the rattle of the wrapper, the chewing, smell the chocolate.

I did not sleep well after my sister left, though I did not sleep terribly well when she was there either, always lurching in and out of dreams, waking to see her staring down at me, or staring at herself in the black mirror. Sometimes I could not tell what I was dreaming and what was real. I often wondered when she slept, and I wanted to ask her, but she would never answer any of my questions directly. Usually she just stared at herself in the mirror as if there were no one else in the room. —I am not happy, she said once, when I asked her some innocuous thing or other.

When she moved into the guest room, she must have slept for days straight, just to catch up on all those years she missed. For days I heard nothing from her room. I was afraid for a while that she had died in there, so silent was she, and I would walk out to the yard to look up, but her window stayed dark. At first I thought she might kill herself, and some nights I used to put myself to sleep imagining her in her room, packing up her things, stacking them in neat piles in the corner, with little notes designating who was to get what. Only later did I realize that this was something that would not even occur to her; rather, it was the kind of thing I myself might do. After that I thought about it sometimes, packing and labeling and stacking all my things against the wall, but then I could never think of what to do next, what would happen to them, or to me. When I thought of my sister doing this, I always imagined my own stack to be the largest, the most carefully chosen, the most personal, and that it would be the last thing she would see before she lay on her back and crossed her arms across her chest, as she had done when we were children. She would look at my box before she died; her last thoughts would be of me.

But this is not how it happened; her things were a mess, my mother told me, her room a shambles. It was just lucky, my mother said, that the fire did not spread beyond my sister's bed. I wake and sleep throughout the night; Jerome is like a face without eyes in the ghostly light of the television, Debbie an inert little lump at my feet. I wonder what it is she dreams of if she dreams: perhaps the touch of her owner's hand, her owner's voice, her owner's lonely life without her.

Somewhere outside, circus animals are shivering in the dark; the fields are too wide, too open. Elephants tremble.

Danny smiles at me from across the room, moves toward me, reaches for me in a wooden embrace; he leaves a baby in my arms, and I feel the wooden tug of its mouth at my breast, and hear the wooden click of its teeth. My breasts turn to wood as it sucks, my breasts and my lips, my hands and skin—all wood.

I open my eyes to a gloomy morning light, then close them. I am cold and stiff from Danny's wooden touch. I remind myself that he is not here; he is at home, in his bed; his sheets are snug around his chin and he is dreaming of the beautiful future, a world full of live girls. I am no longer in his dreams and with every moment that passes he is forgetting me. Only when I rise and see Jerome in the bed next to me, and Debbie at the foot of my own, do I remember that Danny is nothing more than ashes, a pile of ashes in a burnt ruined city; he will scatter at the first morning breeze.

Live girls

. . .

Outside in the parking lot are the sounds of voices, hushed in the early morning, and the scraping of frost from windows; cars start, crackle away over the frosty pavement. Take me with you, I think; take us all. There is not one of us that does not need saving.

Jerome moans as I pull open the curtains. He lifts his sleeping mask and peers out at me, then lets it snap back over his eyes.

—Oh my, he says. —If I've died and gone to Heaven, send me back.

—It's not Heaven, I say. —It's New Jersey. This is really only a guess on my part; I stopped watching signs sometime yesterday when they started to seem something like roadkill—just one more thing you don't want to look at by the side of the road.

Jerome sighs. —Don't you look at me, he says. —I'm a fright.

And he is—makeup has rubbed away from his face, leaving his puffy skin exposed in bluish bruised patches. He pulls the mask from his eyes again, and peers out.

—Are you looking at me? he asks.

I turn to the window. —No, I say. —I was watching the traffic. Early as it is, the highway is already busy. Somewhere circus animals are shivering under an unfamiliar sky. Already they miss the other animals, and they are confused with longing for the hand of the trainer they hated. They will roam the suburbs until they are caught or killed, stealing from quiet yard to quiet yard, making meals of pets, frightening children.

I turn back to the room; Jerome has pulled the covers over his head and lies completely still, like a body in a morgue, until suddenly he rises and goes to the bathroom, pulling his covers with him, like a robe around his shoulders, leaving little smears of blue and red and brown on his pillow.

Outside, people carry things to their cars—suitcases, coolers, boxes filled with presents. I have nothing to pack, so I put Jerome's empty suitcase on his bed. All of his dresses seem to be made of the same silky material; the one I hold up to myself is blue, with tiny yellow dots, not a very good color for me, but even so, with one hand holding up my hair, I can see how nice I could look. For just a moment, I don't resemble my mother or my sister or even myself; for a moment I look like someone else. The girl I see, the woman, could not be such a hard person to love. Perhaps this is the girl Danny saw when he watched me from across the room. I turn my head to the side, and look at the line of my neck just as Jerome cracks open the door and peers out.

—I thought I heard you out there, he says. —You put that back. I told you those was for Hollywood.

He glares at me until I have hung up his dress and sat on the end of my bed; then he closes the door. I lie back, with my head close to Debbie. When she doesn't move, I edge closer, so that my face is just next to her. Her body moves as she breathes; with each breath her fur brushes my skin.

The television is still on, but the sound is off; it's a religious show. A man paces back and forth across a stage, preaching to a large audience; behind him a line of men and women wait, watching him, until suddenly he turns and calls one over. A woman approaches, her face a shining beacon of trust; the man turns, says something to her, then puts his hand on her head. Her eyes flutter, then close, and she swoons, but as she falls back, two men appear at her side, catching her smoothly, laying her gently on the floor; another woman comes forward and places a small towel over her legs, which are exposed to the audience. The man goes through the same routine with a few more people from the line on the stage—talks to them, touches them, stands back while they swoon to the floor. I turn the sound up as he approaches the remaining people on the stage.

—Jesus, he is saying, —Jesus, Jesus, and he walks up and down the line, dispensing with the conversation entirely, instead simply laying his hands on people's heads, and one by one they fall, like a row of toy soldiers. Then he turns to the camera and speaks to us: What do we need healed? he asks. He promises to send Jesus to heal it. —Just let him in, he instructs, —let him in today.

—That fool, Jerome says behind me, and I turn. He has painted his cheeks bright red, and his lips are like a red gash in his face. I think of him swooning on the stage, falling into the arms of the men there, and Jesus coming down to save him, to wipe away the bruises on his skin, to heal the bright wound of his mouth. —Invest in Heaven, the man on the screen says. —Make Heaven a place for you.

—Heaven, Jerome says. —Let me tell you about Heaven, he says, but then he is silent and sits on the edge of his bed, watching people tumble all across the stage.

—Well, I say, —let's get moving, but he doesn't take his eyes from the television, so I pick Debbie up and carry her outside. A man is standing by the car next to ours, loading suitcases into the trunk; he looks up as I walk past him to put Debbie onto a little patch of grass.

—Nice cat, he says; he lifts a box of presents into the back seat of the car.

I nod. —She's a Christmas present, I say, —for my sister. Debbie looks alarmed at being set on the ground; she flattens herself against the grass and looks nervously around. —She's kind of thin, the man says, and we both stare down at Debbie; after a while she begins to crawl, though it is more like creeping, her stomach only an inch or two from the ground.

—It's the breed, I say. —It's a thin breed. The man nods; a woman stands in a doorway behind him, watching us. After a moment, she calls out to him, and he turns, looks at her, then walks away without another word to me. When I turn around, Debbie is staring at me; I pick her up and settle her in the back of Danny's car.

Jerome is still watching television when I return to the room; he has not moved or dressed or begun to pack.

—Ready? I say from the door, but he waves his arm to quiet me.
—Hush, he says. —Listen. On the screen, a man is standing in a
dark tunnel, holding a microphone and pointing at the wall next
to him, then to the ground. The camera pans down to show a circle of cigarette butts around the man's feet. Then we move to a
motel room, and the camera zooms up to a mirror, the kind of
mirror on every motel wall, the kind of mirror on our own wall
next to the television. The lights go dark and shining through
the mirror is a tiny pinprick of light; the camera stays on it a
long time; then there is a commercial. Jerome turns to me.
—See, he says, —these *men*–he gestures at the television–spy
on people. At their motels.
He shudders as he gets up from the bed. —Now *that* gives me
the creeps, he says. He glances at the mirror as he passes it, then
stops and brings his face close to it, peering all over the glass.
—Hi, honey, he says after a moment, then touches his lips to
the glass in a kiss. He pulls back, leaving a pair of lips shim-
mering on the glass, like a mouth suspended in the air.
—There, he says. —You just been kissed by a movie star. He
winks at me as he walks to the bathroom, snatching a dress
from the closet as he passes it.
I come close to the mirror, and look it over for the kind of pin-
hole in the television show, but the light in the room is too
bright to see through the glass; up close, all I can see are my
own dark pupils, and what they reflect back to me: the beds, the
room, the things we have brought with us. I close my eyes, then
press my mouth to the mirror where Jerome has left his kiss.
The glass is cold, the lipstick waxy, and when I draw back, the
kiss is smeared and my own lips are faintly stained with red.
I lie back on the bed and think of what I would ask to be
healed; I can feel the hand on my head, the swoon, the arms
catching me, lowering me to the floor. And Debbie–Debbie too
would be healed. I reach for her head, listen for her quick
breath; for a moment I can hear it, and feel the soft beat of her

heart beneath her fur; then I remember that she is already in the car. My mouth feels strange and stiff, like a mouth from someone else's face.

When Jerome comes out of the bathroom, he looks at me a long time, as if he cannot place what has changed about me; finally he realizes it is the lipstick, and he nods.
—Well, Miss, he says, —that's an improvement.
I close my eyes again, until he is ready to go; as we leave, I catch a motion in the mirror and turn to see who is there, but it's only our shadows moving across the wall–dark ghosts in the mirror, following us out of the room.

Across from the motel is a little doughnut shop. Jerome stands in line with me, watching as a woman in front of us orders chocolate doughnuts. They are out, the clerk tells her; they just ran out. When it's our turn, Jerome orders a chocolate dough-nut, and when the clerk tells him they are out and asks if he wants something else, he draws up in haughty outrage.
—Honey, he says, —I don't want nothing else. I wanted a choco-late doughnut. He gazes at the wall of doughnuts behind her.
—With sprinkles, he adds, then turns and sulks off to a table by the window, where he sits and stares out at the parking lot.
When I join him, I push my plate across the table, and he stares at my doughnut a long time, then shakes his head.
—I had my heart set on chocolate, he says. He lets out a long aggrieved sigh. —My *heart,* he says.
—You heard that woman say they were out, I say. —You wouldn't have eaten them if they'd had them.
He stares at me. —I might have, he says. —If they had what I wanted, I might have eaten it. He turns his head to gaze out the window.
—When I'm a movie star, he says, —I'm going to have choco-late doughnuts every day. He sighs; the tendons of his neck

look tight enough to snap. He has not eaten since we have been together.

—Oh my, he says. —Would you look at that.

In the parking lot, a man and woman are getting out of their car; the man is nearly as thin as Jerome, but the woman is enormous and she is struggling to get out of her seat. Jerome watches, openmouthed, as they enter the store and walk to the counter.

—Honey, he whispers, —you don't need no doughnuts.

As the man and woman carry their tray to the table next to us, Jerome's eyes slide sideways to watch them, and when the woman takes a bite of her doughnut, he leans over the table to me.

—That's a sin, he says, —that fat old thing eating that doughnut. He turns his head every few seconds to glance at the woman, until finally she realizes she is being watched; the man with her turns around to Jerome, whose eyes are still on the woman.

—Excuse me, Miss? the man says to Jerome, and I stand.

—Let's go, I say, taking Jerome's arm. It feels as dry and light as a stick of driftwood; I could snap it with a hard tug. He jerks it away from me, and stands, snatching his fur from the back of his chair, turning with a little huff. The man half-rises.

—Excuse me, Miss? he says again. The woman watches us without expression; her hand rests on top of her doughnut.

Even when we are in the parking lot, Jerome continues to watch the couple as I take Debbie out of the car and set her on the pavement; she sniffs at the little container of creamer I've brought out for her, and darts her tongue at it a few times, but the angle of it is awkward, and I dribble a bit on my finger, then hold it out to her; she licks it off, and I give her more, and again like this until the cream is nearly gone.

I close my eyes; her tongue on my finger is like a quick little insect, beating its wings against my skin. The sun is warm on my face. Soon we will be in Florida, where we will find a little house by the sea; we will have doughnuts for breakfast every day; we will be as happy as we have always dreamed of being. Nothing will ever happen to surprise us. When I open my eyes, Jerome is watching us; he looks at me a moment longer, then turns his face away.

—That ain't even real cream, he says.

Under the bright sun and a heavy coat of makeup, his face is pale, bleached out; it seems to be disappearing, leaving only the red gash of his mouth. A young man and woman walk past us, holding hands. They pause to kiss, and Jerome and I both watch them pass. The man flashes us a smile when he sees us watching them. Jerome sighs as the couple gets in their car and drives away.

—That's all I want, he says. —Him. Someone just like him.

He gets in the car and turns to watch me settle Debbie.

—That fat old woman, he says. —Someone loves her. He shakes his head. —That greasy old cat.

I run my hand along Debbie's back; her fur ripples in response, then her tail lifts gently, drops gently. Jerome closes his eyes but rouses and looks grumpily around when I pull out of the parking lot.

A boy, maybe seventeen, eighteen, stands at the mouth of the highway, his thumb out, a small knapsack by his feet. —Oooh, Jerome says as we approach. —Oooh, stop for this boy. The boy looks harmless enough, with a pleasant smile even for the cars that pass him by. Jerome slaps at my shoulder.

—Come on, he says. —That boy's getting colder and I ain't getting any younger.

The boy smiles at us both when he gets in the car.

—Hi, honey, Jerome says, and the boy nods, then looks down at Debbie beside him.

—Hey, he says. —A cat. He reaches down to pet her, but Jerome bats at his arm.

—That old cat, he says. —Don't you pay it no attention.

He turns around in his seat and leans his neck out, resting his chin on the back of the seat, gazing at the boy.

—Where y'all headed? the boy asks, and Jerome sighs.

—Y'all, he repeats dreamily. —A Southern boy.

—West, I say. —California.

—Hollywood, Jerome corrects. —We are headed to Hollywood. The boy's eyes meet mine in the mirror. —Hollywood, he says.

—No shit. Y'all gonna be movie stars?

—Yes, Jerome says. —I am. Me.

—No shit, the boy says. His eyes meet mine again in the mirror, linger there. His eyes are so dark I can't distinguish the pupil from the iris. I can see nothing in them. He closes them.

—Well, he says, —if y'all don't mind, I'm going to catch some sleep. He leans his head against the window. Jerome starts to turn back in his seat, then looks again at the boy.

—You know, he says. —I was Miss Black America.

—Huh, the boy says, his eyes fluttering. —How 'bout that. A beauty queen.

He drifts off, and Jerome turns back, beaming. —A beauty queen, he murmurs.

I look at him. —Don't they have to be women? I ask, and he waves his hand dismissively at me.

—Honey, he says, —I am in the middle of nowhere. I can be anything I want. He lowers his visor and moves it so he can see the boy in his mirror. —I could love that boy, he says. —Those blue eyes.

The boy sleeps soundly as we drive, but just his presence has perked Jerome up considerably. Every now and then, he checks on the boy in his mirror, sighs happily, and gazes out the window. I am surprised every time I look in my rearview mirror and see the boy there. Debbie sleeps against his outstretched leg. At some point I turn the radio on, but Jerome snaps it quickly off, and puts his finger to his mouth, with a glance back at the boy. After that, we drive in silence, until we stop for gas. Jerome is out of the car, holding his little cosmetics case, before I've even turned the engine off. He leans back in his window as the boy's eyes open.

—Don't you forget me, he says to the boy. The boy nods groggily, and watches me fill up the tank, then leans forward, his arms over the seat, as I park by the service area.

—You're kind of an unusual pair, he says.

I nod. —I guess so, I say.

—I mean you being white and all, he says. He is leaning too close for me to see him in the mirror, but I can smell him next to me, a kind of funky boy smell from days spent on the road. I turn off the engine.

—I'm going to get some coffee, I say, and he gets out and walks along with me.

—I didn't mean nothing by that, he says. —Just y'all are kind of unusual.

—You mentioned that, I say, looking around for the coffee shop.

—I was just wondering, you know, how you got to be friends, is all.

His smile is fake, oily; I am his ride and he wants to keep me.

—We're sisters, I tell him, and he takes a step back.

—Oh, he says. —Sorry.

—It's okay, I say. —No one can tell. We're adopted. Our parents died when we were very young.

The boy looks shocked and sorry and impressed, all at once.

—No shit, he breathes, and I nod as Jerome comes out of the women's room. His hair is teased to nearly a foot above his head. Half his face seems to be his mouth, his bright-red lips. He spots us and comes over, smiling at the boy.

—Wow, the boy says, looking up at him. —You sure are tall.

Jerome giggles coyly and the boy looks at me. I turn and walk into the coffee shop. I find a booth and slide in; Jerome waits for

the boy to sit across from me, then slides in right up next to
him. I can see a strip of stubble from Jerome's jawline to his
collar. It is on the other side of his neck from the boy, but when
the waitress comes, the boy inches away from Jerome and in-
spects him closely, his face, his neck. Jerome is happily ordering food, some sort of diet plate, and when he is done, he drops
his menu and turns to the boy, who orders a huge meal of eggs,
toast, sausage, bacon. Jerome looks faintly disgusted at each
new item.

—Honey, he says, —you're going to blow up with all that food.

—Yeah, the boy says, —well, I ain't eaten in a while.

He seems less good-humored than when we picked him up. His
eyes follow the waitress as she walks away. —Cute little butt, he
says, and Jerome puts his hand over the boy's.

—She's nothing, Jerome says. —She's just trash.

The boy looks down at Jerome's hand, huge even for a tall
woman, and Jerome pulls it suddenly away and puts both hands
in his lap, but the boy leans back now and scrutinizes him
openly; his face changes with the realization, and he shakes his
head.

—You ain't no woman, he says, and Jerome looks startled,
bringing his hands to his face, then dropping them again in his
lap. He looks away, out at the room.

—I am, he says. —I am a woman. I'm a beauty queen.

The boy looks at me, and shakes his head again, as if I am responsible for this, as if he somehow expected better from me.
He reaches under the table for his knapsack and slides sideways, bumping into Jerome, then waiting until Jerome gets up.
The boy looks up at him as he gets out, then back at me.

—Y'all're freaks, he says. —Both of y'all are freaks.

Jerome watches him walk out, then sits again, his eyes straight
ahead. From here, I can see the boy walk across the parking lot,
headed back to the highway. When the waitress returns with
our food, she sets the boy's plate down at his place, though she

180-181

has probably seen him leave, then slaps a bill down at the edge
of the table. Jerome watches her walk away; he looks down at
his food, a nicely arranged assortment of things like carrot
sticks and orange slices, with a round white lump of cottage
cheese in the middle. He pushes the plate away and stands.

—I'll be waiting in the car, he says and holds his hand out for
the keys. I look up at him. He could leave me here; he could
take Debbie from the back seat and leave her on the pavement;
he could drive off and find that boy, and together they could go
to Hollywood. I hand him the keys and watch him walk across
the room like a queen, as though all eyes are on him, as though
everyone in the room is admiring him.

Across from me sit two perfect, untouched plates of food, staring back at me like dining companions. The boy's food smells
of meat and grease, and when I take a bite of my sandwich, it
tastes like meat and grease. I push it away and finish my coffee.
A little receptacle by the salt and pepper holds a stack of postcards–all pictures of the restaurant we're in. It's described on
the back with words like "friendly" and "discriminating" and
"delicious," as if someone who got this postcard might want to
make a trip just to come here to eat. I take the pen provided
with the cards.

Dear, I write, then stop. *Mother,* I think, *Father.* Even when I
close my eyes, I cannot see their faces, only the vague shapes of
people in chairs. *Danny,* I think, then *Dave,* but they are ashes
behind me. Everyone is ashes behind me. If I had someone to
send this card to, I think of what I would write: *Debbie is
dying,* I would say. *Jerome has not eaten for two days. I am all
alone.*

I leave the card unaddressed. *We will be there soon,* I write. *We
are having a wonderful time.* Next to the cashier is a small
mailbox, and after I pay for the food, I slip the card into it. Our
waitress takes my money, and glances at me, then at our table,
where our food sits nearly untouched.

• • •

Jerome does not look at me when I get in the car. He stares straight ahead as I pull out of the parking lot, then watches the road closely when we reach the highway. The boy is nowhere in sight; he has already been picked up by someone else. After a while, Jerome lays his head down, his back to me; it is warm enough now that he doesn't need the cover of his coat, but he draws it up over his shoulders.

I drive all day; the road is like a snake unwinding in front of us, and the landscape rises around us as we approach it, disappears as we leave it behind; all that exists is what I can see. Debbie is curled up tightly in back, and Jerome murmurs, wakes, drifts off again. As we travel south, insects fly against the car, splatting in little blotches against the windshield. I drive until it grows dark and the sky is like a black wall around us. I feel as if I am driving into a cave. *Come to me,* my sister calls. She rises like an owl at the furthest mouth of the cave. Her wings spread across the sky, the road, the whole earth, and just as they close around us, I jerk awake, with a sudden swerve of the wheel. Jerome stirs and looks around.

—Girl, he says. —Watch yourself. I keep my eyes on the tail-lights of the truck ahead of us, until I find a place to stop.

By the time I park and get Debbie inside, Jerome is already undressing; he turns as I enter and lifts his robe up to cover his body.

—Excuse me? he says. —A little privacy? I put Debbie on the bed he has left empty.

—Can't you use the bathroom? I ask, and he rolls his eyes.

—There's about two feet of room in there, he says. —I need my space.

Past the parking lot, across the street, is a little convenience store; when I ask Jerome if he wants anything, he just raises his eyebrows and holds the robe up until I leave the room. It takes only a few minutes to get to the store and back; as I approach our room, I can see Jerome through a slit in the curtains. He is standing at the sink, in his robe; his back is to me, and I can see his face as he looks at himself. He can't be more than twenty feet away from me. As I watch, he drops his robe. He is all bones and hollows and his ribs and back are blotted with the fading shadows of bruises.

He turns his head from side to side, then picks up a can of shaving cream, and sprays it over his chest and face until he is covered in a big puffy cloud. He pulls a razor slowly over his face and his neck, and when he has finished, he stops and looks down at himself; after a long moment, he opens the razor and takes the blade out, then holds it almost delicately to his chest. His shoulders lift and fall in a long sigh; then he closes his eyes and draws the razor blade across his chest. A thin line of blood rises through the cloud of shaving cream, following the motion of his hand, bright red on white, like blood in snow. Past him in the mirror, I can see Debbie's reflection, a tight little mound on the bed, exactly as I left her.

I turn and walk to the car. Every station on the radio is talk; all voices, all of them unhappy, disappointed. A man on one station calls to say his wife is unfaithful; he has given her everything, he says; what can he do? On another station, a woman says her children do not love her; what has she done wrong? she asks, what could she have done differently? As they talk, people everywhere are reaching for their own phones, and I lean back and close my eyes. The window is down, and the warm night air is like a blanket over me.

I am lost, I want to say to the man on the radio, I am lost, and I am driving into a long black tunnel, and I have nothing but a cat and a companion and both of them are dying. How did this happen? I would ask him; what did I do wrong? What could I have done differently? Leave them, the man on the radio says. Leave them and drive away. Don't even think about looking back. Come to me, he says, and the voice is my sister's: *Come to me.*

Where I am is the deepest part of the deepest cave. Where I am there is nothing but my sister's voice, and everywhere the rustle of spiders. *I am here,* she says. *We are here forever.* Her hand is a spider on my throat; her hand is a spider across my breast, a spider in my mouth.

When I open my eyes, I do not know if I have been asleep or awake. The woman in the cave said that after she had been underground for a few months, sometimes she could not tell what was a waking thought from what was a dream; when she lay down to go to sleep at night, she was often confused about what was going to happen, what it would mean. She had trouble after a while, she said, telling what was real. At first this bothered her, but gradually she found it comforting; she said it made her feel less responsible for things, and by the time she left the cave, it had ceased to be a problem; but when she was back aboveground, she would find herself looking at her hand, for example, and thinking: Whose hand is this? But whereas it had not bothered her in the cave, where she was now it seemed to matter. That was the worst of it, she said, that it seemed to matter. I snap the radio off and carry the bag of food to the room. It's early enough that most of the windows in the motel are lit, and while nearly all of them have the curtains drawn, here and there a few are open. I glance in at them as I pass; in a room a few doors down from ours, a man sits on the edge of his bed, talking on the telephone. He looks up and sees me out here, looking in at him; he meets my eyes and continues talking as he watches me. I realize after a moment that he is crying. We look at each other a long time, but if we meet in the parking lot in the morning, we will probably not recognize each other's faces. His eyes move to follow me as I walk away.

Jerome is dressed in a pair of silky pajamas when I come back into the room; they are buttoned to the throat, and he is

perched at the end of his bed, watching the news on television.
I lay out the food I've bought: a package of cupcakes, a little
carton of cream, a can of wax beans. Jerome stares at the food
a moment, then looks back at the television, where a weatherman is tracking the course of a winter snowstorm that is a day
or so behind us, following us south. Where we have been is bitter cold and snow; it seems impossible that it could catch up to
us. Somewhere in those storms behind us, elephants plod
through snowdrifts; tigers and lions lift their paws to shake off
snow, put them down, and lift to shake them again. They are
not used to winter. They are not used to open fields. They
are not used to anything that is happening to them now.

The weatherman moves back and forth in front of his map; he
is tall and blond and perfect; Jerome watches him as he warns
holiday travelers of heavy snowdrifts along the highways.

—I'd like to get you in a snowdrift, Jerome says.

When the weather report ends, he lies back on his bed.

—I'm going to meet someone just like that in Hollywood, he
says. —He's going to sweep me off my feet.

—He's a weatherman, I say. —You'd have to talk about the
weather all the time.

Jerome looks at me sideways. —Honey, he says, —we wouldn't
talk. He sighs. —We would be just too beautiful to talk. He
closes his eyes and smiles dreamily. —We're going to have one
of those big mansions, he says. —With a swimming pool. And
a special little room to watch movies in. Everything will be
made of gold. He is quiet a moment.

—Everything will be made of gold, he repeats.

When the sports comes on, he sits up and changes the channel,
then stands and looks at the food I've brought. As I pour a little cream into a cup for Debbie, he picks up the can of wax
beans; he stares at the label a long time, moving his finger back
and forth over the information on the back. Finally, he puts it
down.

—I didn't know it was so many calories, he says.

Debbie laps up most of the cream I give her; she is looking better, I tell myself, and when I run my hand up and down her back, I am sure she is softer, cleaner, a little less thin. When I look up, Jerome is standing in the center of the room watching us; the look on his face is something like hunger. He turns to the mirror as our eyes meet, but I can see in his reflection that he is still watching us. I bend my head to Debbie.

—Debbie, I say. —Debbie, we're going to Hollywood.

—She don't know what you mean, Jerome says. —That poor old cat. He turns up the sound on the television and lies back on his bed, pulling his sleep mask from the pocket of his robe.

—Lord, he says. —I never been so tired.

He arranges his mask over his eyes, then lays his hands across his chest. In only a moment he is breathing deeply. After a little while, I stand over him.

—Jerome, I say in a conversational tone, then again, but there is no answer. The bruise on his cheek is fading, and his skin is clean-shaven down to his robe, which is buttoned up around his neck. His skin looks soft, delicate, fragile.

—Jerome, I say again, and he stirs, but does not wake.

I turn off the television, and then the lights, and lie down next to Debbie, on top of my covers. Outside in the parking lot, cars arrive and circle the lot. Their headlights flood our room for a moment with light, then leave us in darkness. As each car passes, I turn to look at Jerome, but always the light is gone too fast, and I cannot see him. I am not sure I remember what it is he looks like. The woman in the cave wrote early on in her diary that she never wanted to see her husband's face again, that he could let her do something like this, but after several months she sometimes forgot she was married at all, and for long stretches the only face she could picture in her mind was that of her mother, who had died in childbirth and whom she had never seen. Sometimes, she looked at the picture she had brought of her husband and remembered with a shock that she was married; at other times, she did not recognize him, but hated him without knowing exactly why, knowing only that he had done something to her. After a while, the picture confused her, and she tore it into tiny pieces, which she then burned. Without good ventilation, she wrote, it seemed as if she was breathing smoke for days, and after that she looked at the little pile of ashes and thought: There was something there that I loved.

She often woke in the morning, looked around her, and thought that she must be being punished, to be left alone in such a place. Sooner or later, she used to tell herself, someone would have to come and take her out of there. She could not remember what it was she had done wrong.

I open my eyes to the rattle of cellophane; Jerome is standing at the table in front of the mirror, and as my eyes adjust to the light, I can see him unwrap the cupcakes and bring them to his face; his reflection in the mirror is ghostly, like someone behind the glass watching him, mimicking his motions. He breathes in deeply, then wraps the cupcakes up again and replaces them on the table. I close my eyes as he returns to his bed, but instead I feel him come and stand above me. I can hear his breath; I can hear the beating of his heart, and for a moment I can feel his hand on my face, but then his bed shifts with the weight of his body as he lies down. I have not felt anything at all.

A car parks outside our room, its lights stalling in the mirror. Even as I tell myself it's a trick of the light—just glass and shadows—I can see there is someone in the mirror, someone watching us as we pretend to sleep. He is in a narrow tunnel behind the wall, his eye pressed to the hole he's drilled there, and he lights cigarette after cigarette, dropping them at his feet. Soon he is standing in a circle of fire; he is burning. He is on fire with wanting. The flames spread, to our wall, our mirror, our bed. I try to move my legs, but they are made of wood, and they will not move. My sister beats her wings, beats her wings; they are in flames and fall to the ground like tiny bits of burning paper. My wooden arms lie at my side. I cannot save us. My face is the last to burn, and as I turn to ash, there is a motion behind the mirror, a hand moving; it is Danny. He dips his hand into his bag of popcorn and brings it to his mouth, chewing as he watches us burn.

In the morning, when I open my eyes, the television is already on, but Jerome is nowhere in sight. I nearly trip over him as I come around the beds to go to the bathroom; he is lying on his back, doing sit-ups along with a woman on the television. He pretends not to see me.
—One hundred sixty-two, he says, barely pulling himself up off the floor. He looks as if he might snap in half, and as I step over him, he swats halfheartedly at my leg.
He is lying flat on his back when I come out of the bathroom, staring up at the ceiling.

The parking lot is busy with people packing up their cars, getting an early start on the day's drive. Debbie and I sit in the cool grass watching them.

When I come back into the room, Jerome has moved to the bed, in front of the television. He is holding the can of wax beans, and his robe has fallen open at his chest; I can see a long dark cut across the skin there, and all around it are more of them, thin dark scars, like little check marks in the skin.
Jerome looks up to see me looking at him, and our eyes meet for a moment; then he pulls his robe closed and looks back at the television. As I turn from him, something moves behind the mirror, something that is not me.
—Let's go, I say to Jerome. —We want to get an early start.

Live girls

He stares at the television, then looks at me a long moment.
—What? he says.

I close the door behind Jerome as we leave; he carries his suitcase to the car, stopping once to let it rest against his legs, then
dragging it the rest of the way. From the back, with his fur coat
over his shoulders and skinny stick legs tottering on his heels,
he looks like a fading movie queen. When he gets to the car, he
leans back against it, closing his eyes a moment, then turning
to look around the parking lot. A few cars over, a young boy
tries to shove a suitcase into an already crammed trunk; Jerome
stares at the boy's straining back and butt and legs.
—Hey, honey, he says. —You come over here. When the boy
finishes with the suitcase and heads back to his room, Jerome
closes his eyes again, his face to the sun; his lips are moving
slightly, but he jerks at the sound of Debbie's door closing, and
turns to look at me, gazing at me as if mine is a face he has
never seen before, but somehow knows he ought to recognize.

Scenery passes, changing like postcards sent from stages in a
journey. Jerome watches it go by.
—We better be getting there soon, he says, not looking away
from the window. —I can't be driving like this forever.
—Tomorrow, I say, though we will be in Florida by tonight.
Jerome leans his head back.
—Tomorrow, he says. —Tomorrow is the first day of the rest of
my life. He lowers his visor and fiddles with the mirror, then sits
back, looking straight at it; he sits that way for miles, just gazing at himself, long enough for the light to change as the sun
slides behind clouds across the sky.
—You poor old cat, he says after a while, and I realize he has
been looking at Debbie all this time, not at himself. He turns
around in his seat and gazes at her directly, then shakes his head.

—You wouldn't be so bad if you was fixed up, he says. He sighs, then turns around in his seat and goes back to watching the scenery. The way he's arranged his mirror, what I can see of him in it is his torso and his hand restlessly moving over himself, picking at a thread, then suddenly smoothing it down, sliding over his ribs, pinching at his waist and thighs. His nail polish has chipped away from his fingernails; some has flecked onto the skin, like tiny bright drops of blood.

We ride in silence most of the day. I can tell Jerome is awake by his restlessness and by an occasional impatient sigh, but he says nothing until I stop at a roadside rest stop, and then only when I try to follow him into the women's room. He puts his hand gently on my chest.

—Girl, he says, —nothing against you, but I got to be alone.

In the parking lot, people in cars, most of them families, bustle in and out of the little building, but the truckers seem in no hurry at all; they stand together by their row of trucks, smoking and talking. One of them walks past Debbie and me; he is wearing bright mirrored sunglasses and as he looks down at us, our tiny images jiggle in his glasses. Jerome comes out of the women's room; he is walking a little shakily, but as the trucker passes him, he straightens and turns.

—That's a nice cat, someone says, and I look up. A woman is bent over, her hand held out to Debbie, who sniffs it, then puts her head back on her paws. I nod.

—She just needs a little fixing up, I say. The woman smiles, then walks to a car and opens the back door to remove a small cooler, which she carries across the grass to a picnic table; a man and two children are already there. It's like a television commercial. I lie back on the warm grass.

—Debbie, I whisper, but she doesn't even look at me. I don't know if she would recognize my face or my voice or the touch of my hand. When I reach for her, she stiffens, then relaxes as I pet her. I had thought she was looking better–cleaner, less skinny–but really she is nothing but bone and a little scraggly fur, and when she looks at me, there is hardly a flicker in her eyes. She is going to die here.

I carry her over to our car and open the trunk. Jerome is nowhere in sight. I pull out his suitcase. It pops open, letting out the smell of sweat and perfume. From the jumble of silky clothes I untangle a scarf I've seen Jerome wear, a blue-and-green strip of satin with little sparkling stars, and I tie it gently around Debbie's neck. It gives her a festive look, like something someone would want, perhaps even love. The woman who spoke to me is busy with her family; none of them are looking at us, and no one else pays any attention as I carry Debbie to their car and settle her against a pillow in the back seat.

—Debbie, I say, and she looks at me. —This will make you happy.

Little stars sparkle in the fur around her neck.

Jerome is not in the women's bathroom, and when I stand out-side the men's room, trying to get a glimpse inside, all I can see is yellow tile. Finally, I find him in back of the building; his fur coat is in a heap on the ground, and he is kneeling in front of the trucker who passed me earlier; the trucker moves his hands over Jerome's head, his neck, down onto his shoulders. The trucker's face is turned to me, but his eyes are masked by the mirrored glasses, and all I can see is a blurry reflection of trees and bright sky.

In the bathroom, women and girls stand at the long mirror, washing their hands, combing their hair, applying makeup. I stand with them a moment to wash my hands. There is a mirror on the wall behind us, reflecting this one, so that in front of me there are rows and rows of faces, thousands of girls watching themselves watch themselves.

Jerome is already in the car when I come out of the bathroom; he is wearing the trucker's mirrored sunglasses, and as I walk toward the car, I can see myself coming closer. He waves and I watch myself lift my arm to wave back.

—Yoo-hoo, sweetheart, he says, and I drop my arm when I realize it is not me he is looking at. I turn and see the trucker behind me. He ignores Jerome.

—Humph, Jerome says as I get in the car. —He liked me just fine a minute ago. He watches the trucker climb into the cab of his truck—it's a livestock carrier, crammed so full that I can't identify the animals from the little bubbles of flesh that poke out through the slats.

—Oh my, Jerome says. —A animal truck.

He gasps suddenly and brings his hands to his face, inhaling deeply.

—Do I smell like animals? he asks, and holds his hands to my face.

Almost all his nail polish has chipped away, and the nail of his index finger is shredded. I breathe in. There is an animal smell, cows or pigs, but I say no, and he sniffs at his hands again himself.

—That cat's bad enough, he says, but animals is just too much. He lowers his visor, then roots around in his purse, and pulls out makeup—compact, lipstick, a little bottle of perfume. He holds the perfume up and sprays it into the air above his head. It sparkles in the light.

As we drive away, the family I've left Debbie with is finishing their picnic; they're wrapping things up, throwing garbage away. A small girl waits beside the car for the rest of them. Debbie will be hers, I think; she will sleep at the foot of her bed every night, and during the day she will doze on the ledge of a sunny window.

Jerome pulls down his visor and looks at himself in the mirror, then sighs and opens the compact. He pats powder heavily over his face and throat; patches of stubble are visible even through the powder, at his jawline and over the rise of his Adam's apple. He smears lipstick unevenly over his mouth, then drops the cosmetics on the seat next to him and leans back. I can't tell if his eyes are closed or open. His glasses reflect only his mirrored face in the visor. I find myself every now and then glancing in the rearview mirror for Debbie. Every time I see the empty back seat, I feel a quick surge of panic, as if I have left something important behind.

Without Debbie, there is nothing for me to do when we reach a motel, so I sit on my bed and watch Jerome stumble in with his suitcase. This room is exactly like the others we have stayed in, but it will be our last; I have only fifteen or twenty dollars left—not enough for another room. Jerome drops his suitcase and turns on the television; he switches channels until he finds a talk show, then sits down heavily on the edge of his bed. It is dark, but he is still wearing the trucker's sunglasses. The television makes two bright squares in each lens. On the show, a circle of women are sitting in front of an audience; one of them is talking about her marriage, which seems little more than a string of infidelities her husband committed before he finally left her. Jerome shakes his head in sympathy, with a few gentle tsks.

—I don't know what I could have done, the woman says, —how I could have made him stay.

—Well, honey, Jerome says, —you could try fixing yourself up. He turns and looks at me. —Speaking of which, he says, then stops.

—What? I ask.

—Well, he says, —I don't mean to be rude, but you've been wearing them same clothes every day. Didn't you bring nothing?

—I did, I say. —It's in the car.

—Uh-huh, he says. —Well, a change of scenery wouldn't hurt no one.

He turns back to the television as the show breaks to a commercial for ice cream, and pays no attention as I leave the room.

The clothes in my sister's box are mostly practical things— sweaters, a jacket, even socks. Because I did not see my sister for so long before she died, almost none of these things are familiar; not until I reach the bottom of the box do I find something I recognize—the bathrobe she wore for years, made of soft blue material with a pattern of red and yellow butterflies. Sometimes as she moved around our room at night, the light outside would catch the butterflies as if they were in flight; I used to close my eyes and imagine them fluttering across the room to light on my face, hundreds of them, so that my face was nothing but a cloud of darkness and beating wings.

Jerome is lying down when I come back into the room; he is still in his clothes, still wearing the glasses, but his mouth is slightly open, his head turned away from the television. He is completely still, and I watch him for a long time before I can detect the slight rise and fall of his chest. His face is all garish smears of makeup, and his neck is crisscrossed with tiny knicks and bumps from shaving. I lay my sister's robe over him, and turn off the television and all the lights, but when I lie down on my own bed, I cannot sleep; I cannot even close my eyes.

Across from me the mirror shifts and stirs with every move I make, and finally I rise. Jerome's fur lies across the desk in front of the mirror, and as I climb up to hang it over the glass, my sister's face appears next to my own.

Come to me, she whispers. *Come. I will save you*, she says.

The glass is like a cool hand against my cheek, and all night I feel the soft pulse of her wings as she holds me in the dark cave of her arms.

I wake to a gloomy dawn, my cheek pressed against the glass, Jerome's fur around my shoulders. I pull away from the mirror; my face is flat white and drawn. Jerome is on his side, turned away from me, still covered by my sister's robe; he does not wake at the soft click his cosmetic case makes when I open it. I turn back to the mirror, and look at my face a moment, then make the first dark mark across my mouth.

When I've finished, I kneel by Jerome's bed.

—Jerome, I say, then again, and again, louder, but he does not respond, and I feel a faint panic rising. He cannot leave me now, I think. We have come so far, and we have left so much behind us.

I take his shoulder and shake him softly, and finally he stirs and turns his face to me. His eyes flutter open and he stares at me a long time.

—Look at you, he says at last, then closes his eyes, and I shake his shoulder again.

—It's time to get up, I say. —We're here. In Hollywood. They're waiting for us.

—Hollywood? he murmurs, then nods dreamily. He sits up slowly, looking around, and when he sees my sister's robe over his arm, he touches it softly, with one finger, as if it were made of gold.

Jerome gazes in the mirror on his visor as I drive around looking for the ocean.

—You old cat, he says, then turns around to look at the back
seat. He stares at the empty seat a long time, then looks at me.
—That old cat's gone, he says, and I nod. He sighs. —I loved
that old cat. He shakes his head. —And now I'm all alone. Now
I'm a orphan again.
He stares out through the front windshield, twisting the sunglasses around and around in his hands, and he is silent for a
long time; then he leans his head back. He gazes straight up at
the roof of the car.
—Terrible things was done to me, he says after a while. He
reaches up and wipes his hand over his mouth, smearing lipstick over the stubble on his chin.
—Terrible things, he repeats. He turns to me, and I nod. His
skin is the color of ash, and his eyes are like tiny living things
peering out from the deepest part of a cave.

The ocean, when I find it, looks like just another dirty beach,
the same as the one we left; trash flaps across the pavement and
beer cans clatter in the morning wind. Jerome puts his sunglasses on and opens his door, but he does not move until I
come around to his side of the car. He gazes out at the water,
then pulls my sister's robe tightly around his neck and heads
out across the sand, but makes it only a few steps before he
stumbles and falls to his knees.
He turns to look at me. In his glasses I can see myself and behind me the sun, just beginning to rise. I wave at him, and he
lies down on his back. He is still a while, then begins to move
his arms up and down beside him in the sand, the way a child
would make an angel in the snow. Sand slides smoothly away
from the arcing wings at his side. Terrible things are going to
happen to him. Terrible things are going to happen to all of us.
If I leave him now, before too long children would gather
around him in a hushed circle, staring down at his strange face;
then they would run to find their parents. If I leave him now,

tiny crabs would burrow up through the sand to consume him, and what they left behind would turn to ash, and blow off in the wind. If I leave him now, he will be alone; he will fill his pockets with sand and walk into the waves, where the fish will watch him sink, then swim slowly over to feed upon his face.

When I sit down next to him in the sand, he turns; in his glasses my face is huge, my mouth a bright-red gash. Beyond us the waves beat against the shore. We have come so far and this is where we have come. This is where I have brought us. By now, Debbie is in her new home, where she is warm and safe; Danny is in my bubble, staring out through the glass; my parents are watching their television in silence. Everyone I have left has forgotten me by now, and under the black water my sister is drowning. Her wings beat against the floor of the ocean. She is on fire. I close my eyes. I feel as if I have never slept.

When I open my eyes, Jerome's arm is raised above him; his hand is full of sand, and he lets it sift through his fingers down over his body; then when his hand is empty, he drops it to the ground and fills it again, over and over, covering himself with sand. The wings of the butterflies on his robe beat with the motion of his arm. We are alone. If I leave him now, I will save myself from terrible things, but as the waves beat against the shore, I lie back and watch his arm move, like a cloud of butterflies rising and falling, and the bright sand dropping like diamonds in the morning sun.

A NOTE ON THE TYPE

The text of this book was set in Bodoni, a typeface named for Giambattista Bodoni, born at Saluzzo, Piedmont, in 1740. The son of a printer, Bodoni went to Rome as a young man to serve as an apprentice at the press of the Propaganda. In 1768 he was put in charge of the Stamperia reale in Parma by Duke Ferdinand, a position he held until his death in 1813, in spite of many offers by royal patrons to tempt him elsewhere. His earliest types were those imported from the Paris typefoundry of Fournier, but gradually these were superseded by his own designs, which, in the many distinguished books he printed, became famous all over Europe. His later arrangements with the duke allowed him to print for anyone who would employ him, and with the commissions that flowed in he was able to produce books in French, Russian, German, and English, as well as Italian, Greek, and Latin. His *Manuale tipografico,* issued in 1818 by his widow, is one of the finest specimen books issued by a printer/type designer.

Composed by North Market Street Graphics,
Lancaster, Pennsylvania
Printed and bound by Quebecor Printing,
Fairfield, Pennsylvania
Designed by Virginia Tan